BLOOD MOON
RISING

BY
BRYAN KURT DODD

Published by Hemingway Publishers
Cover design by Hemingway Publishers
ISBN: Printed in the United States

Dedication

To my loving wife, my wonderful children, and my cherished friends—your love, encouragement, and unwavering belief in me have been my greatest blessings. This work is a testament to the strength and inspiration you bring to my life.

Acknowledgment

To James, Ollan, Mark, and Justin—thank you for your unwavering support, guidance, and inspiration. Your presence has been a cornerstone throughout this journey, and I am deeply grateful for the roles each of you have played in making this possible.

CONTENTS

About the Author

Nestled in the rolling hills of southeastern Missouri, Bryan Kurt Dodd makes his home with his beloved wife and three lively children. Despite being a successful author with a collection of children's books under his belt, his latest masterpiece, Blood Moon Rising, marks his long-awaited foray into the enchanting realm of fantasy literature.

Preface

Endeavor, if you will, to follow the tumultuous course of this bold narrative, a thrilling conglomeration of mystery, murder, passion, and pain. In these pages, you will be exposed to a profusion of shocking language, scenes of horrendous violence, and enough schlocky grammar to make an English teacher burst into flames and scream.

If you're searching for an escapade in depravity, humor, and debauchery, look no further. If not, step away from the book at once, for it may prove too much. But if such excitement entices you, take heart and commit yourself to this savage story!

Prepare for a wild ride! And remember, you have been forewarned. Let us begin our delightful tale and immerse ourselves in the Land of Dodd.

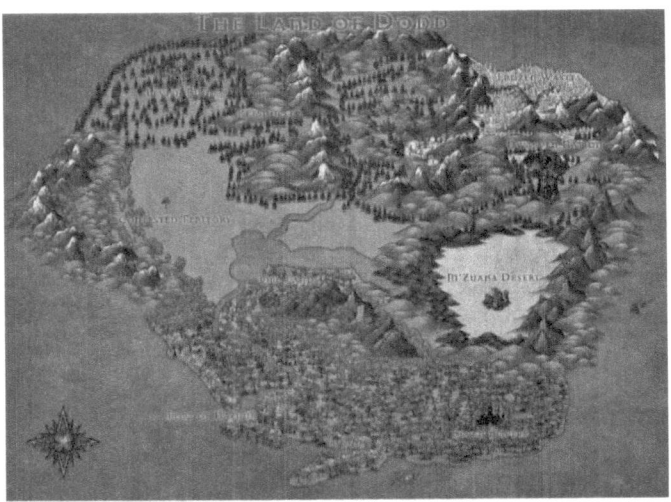

Now, without further ado, let us meet our merry band of assholes. And by a band of assholes, I mean our adventuring band of misfits.

Barnabiz - The ever charismatic, flamboyant ogre bard. I know what you are thinking. Charismatic? Ogre? I am telling you; this guy makes Shrek seem like Grumpy, the dwarf. Why was Grumpy so grumpy, you might ask? You live with a hottie like snow white and share her with six other sex-maddened dwarves. No wonder the guy was always in a foul mood!

One of which is a raging dope fiend. And I heard that little snow could be quite the witch if you catch my drift. And white, who the hell is she trying to fool? That wedding dress will be so black that it will absorb fricking light. But I digress. And by flamboyant, we do mean a bit of a gay. I think he goes every way just to be a little clearer. But just saying the ogre has polished a sword now and again.

Lupine – The quick-witted, razor-tongued goblin rogue who thinks he is a combination of Casanova and Dolomite. Has been known on occasion to partake excessively in dwarven spirits and halfling herb. For those who are unaware, a rogue is a thief. Yes, a thief. A slick-handed, thieving little bastard. And yet, somehow, he always manages to charm his way out of trouble.

Drak - The dragon-born cleric and resident asshole with a heart of gold. For you, dimwitted folk, a cleric is a type of priest, a healer, to be exact. A dragon born is a half-dragon and half-humanoid being. Yep, someone bumped nasties with a dragon.

Damn, we have not even made it out of the preface yet and are already dropping the beastiality bomb. Just remember, you were warned. But alas, here you are. You sick bastards, you. And trust me, the chaos has only just begun.

Auorak - The somewhat human warlock/sorcerer. From henceforth known as the sorcelock. The resident spells chucker of the group, somewhat more of an asshole than the rest of these idiots, and the resident know it all. Okay, he is a massive prick, a major asshole, somewhat of a douche, and an extreme know it all. But hey, every group needs one, right?

Nephrym - The gnome rogue and the other half of our thieving duo. Answers to many names such as powderpuff, fluffy, Mr. Wiggles, gnomekabob, or portable hoe, just to name a few. These will all make sense as the story progresses, trust me. And if they don't, well, that's half the fun, isn't it?

Navine - The minotaur paladin. Protector of the innocent and sometimes our group. She and Justin have been adventuring together for many years.

Every little homo needs their fag hag, it seems. For the less intelligent, a minotaur is a mythical creature that is half human and half cow/bull and a paladin is a badass warrior priest of sorts. And trust me, you do not want to get on her bad side—bullheaded doesn't even begin to cover it.

Chapter 1
It Begins/We Are All Going to Die

The full moon cast its silver glow over the campsite, illuminating every detail in a pale, crimson-hued light. Lupine and Nephrym, exhausted from setting up their temporary home for the night, took a moment to pause and take in their surroundings.

The campfire flames danced and leaped, casting a warm glow across the campsite. The wood crackled and popped, almost in tune with the rustling leaves of the forest. The shadows stretched and twisted, creating an eerie yet somewhat comforting atmosphere.

The harsh wilderness had taken its toll on Nephrym, Lupine, and the rest of the group these last few days. They hadn't seen a hint of civilization in weeks and their stores of even the most basic amenities were dwindling.

Hunger had begun to gnaw at their stomachs and fatigue started to weigh heavy upon their shoulders. Even the gentle rustling of the wind in the trees seemed to lull them into a deeper sense of weariness as the promise of a restful night beckoned to them just beyond the flickering firelight.

"Well, it looks like we have officially made our way into the damp and smelly asshole of the Land of Dodd. I swear to the Gods if I have to ride behind the ogre tomorrow, I am going to cut someone. Starting with the ogre!" Lupine sighed as he yelled, ever so ungracefully plopping himself onto a log beside the fire, clearly worn out from the long day.

"Go ahead, try it, pipsqueak," Barnabiz's voice was thick with malice, and his hand hovered menacingly over his weapon. "I'll make sure you never reproduce again, you pathetic, little goblin scum. And since we are all famished, I'll cook up a stew with your shriveled manhood and your wee little balls as the main ingredient and feed it to ya." He grinned wickedly, eyes glittering with twisted pleasure at the thought of inflicting such brutal punishment upon someone.

"How can you guys continuously keep incessantly bitching? It is absolutely beautiful out here. Look at that sky." Auorak gestured towards the canopy of star-stippled night above them, "These magnificent trees, wildflowers, even the air itself – it's like it is all teaming with magic. I can feel it everywhere," he said in awe.

Lupine raised an eyebrow, his voice dripping with skepticism and curiosity, "I thought only those druid folk fornicated with trees and shit like that?" Lupine looked at the young magic user standing in front of him, his black robes flowing with the night breeze.

Nephrym's words were barely audible over the crackling of the fire as he plopped down on a log. He pulled out his water skin and took a long swig, grimacing at the metallic taste of it before passing it to his goblin companion.

"This forest gives me the creeps, " he said with a shiver. "That ogre gets more and more twisted by the day. I wouldn't be surprised if he started trying to cook and eat you, Lupine." Nephrym shook his head in disgust as he reached for a piece of dried meat from his pack, opting for a more natural and safe meal option. "It is no secret that you're one of his favorite people."

"Never mock an old ogre recipe until you try it. You would like it and it would be your wee goblin friend's man bits it was made from," Barnabiz grumpily remarked. "So that should tell ya something. And I do have a few old ogre recipes for succulent roast gnome."

The ogre and goblin sat at the campfire. Their battle-worn weapons lay at their feet as they both began to clean and sharpen them, as did the rest of the group. They had been through countless battles together, each fight forging a stronger bond between them. As the full crimson moon rose behind them, they knew that no matter what challenges lay ahead, they had each other's back.

The campfire continually crackled and popped, filling the dark night with warmth and light. Auorak sat on a log, his thoughts drifting as he watched the flames dance. The strong scent of smoke filled his nostrils as he reached for another log and placed it carefully onto the fire, causing a spray of sparks to fly into the air.

As the wood caught and the fire grew larger, Auorak felt a sense of peace wash over him. Suddenly, a rustling in the nearby bushes broke the silence, and Auorak's muscles tensed. He turned his head towards the sound, listening intently for any signs of danger. His hand instinctively moved to his staff, eyes scanning the shadows for any movement, heart pounding in anticipation.

Auorak leans in close to his colleagues, trying to be heard over Lupine's incessant chatter. "Shh, I think there's something in the bush over there, just off the trail," he whispered urgently. His eyes darted towards the rustling bushes, and a surge of adrenaline coursed through his body.

Drak's brows furrowed as he cautiously asked, "What are you talking about?" His heart raced with a mix of alarm and excitement, his half-dragon heritage stirring within him.

This spurred Lupine to begin spewing useless chatter again. It took a moment for Auorak to get everyone quiet so he could explain once more.

Auorak's voice cut through the tense silence, sharp and urgent. Lupine flinched at the harshness as Auorak scolded him, "Shut up, you dolt!" His eyes darted around, scanning the forest for any signs of danger. "There's something out there watching us."

"Something watching us?" Lupine loudly fired back. "Who would want to watch you lot? I mean, watch me, I understand," he scoffed.

The rustling noises in the bushes went louder and more urgent, sending a chill up their spines. Whoever or whatever lurks in the shadows knew they were aware of their presence and were getting closer with every passing second. Anxiousness gripped the party like an icy vice as they held their breath in anticipation of what was to come.

"Still, I do not think anything, or anyone, would just want to sit in the forest and watch you all," Lupine exclaimed.

"And if for whatever reason they somehow did not hear this fucked up menagerie of ours as they were coming, they sure as hell do now!" Drak remarked with a disappointed look on his face, staring a hole through Lupine.

Desperation set in like a thick fog. Drak desperately needed action, and he knew whatever or whoever was lurking about could provide it. The cleric had never condoned injustice and villainy. Instead, he always chose to take matters into his own hands, craving only bloodshed to avenge those who deserved justice.

As painful words seemed to compel him to act, our hero felt a rush of adrenaline like never before. It was as if the gods themselves were speaking to him. This may be but a battle for them but also the beginning of the war.

A war they did not even know they had become a part of. A war in which the fate of the entire Land of Dodd was at stake. He felt a heavy weight on his shoulders, the burden of responsibility pressing down as the gravity of their situation sank in.

The adventurers braced for battle as swarms upon swarms of kobolds, their scaly hides gleaming in the campfire's light and moonlight, pouring from the forest like angry ants from an anthill.

The muck and mire on their scales told tales of nights spent huddled in damp and dark caves and beneath fallen tree trunks. They hissed and screeched with rage-filled eyes that glowed with evil intent.

Though they were loathsome and fearful to look upon, our heroes were unable to help but felt a passing sense of disgust seeing them charged into the clearing and into their camp.

The Kobolds Attack!

"Navine, take a left!" Nephrym shouted from his position atop the paladin's backpack as he released a fury of arrows, piercing the skull of one of the diminutive kobolds and impaling another through the chest. They collapsed to the ground, and three more of them followed suit to take their place. Navine swung her massive war hammer in one powerful movement and killed all three with one heavy blow. Splatting them like overripe fruit as kobold bits and pieces flew everywhere.

After Navine and Nephrym moved away, six more emerged from the bushes only to end up charred by Auorak's spell. A mixture of red, blue, and black arcane fire engulfed them instantly, the smell of burning kobold flesh now lingering in the air akin to the acrid odor of death. Their shrieks echoed through the night, a haunting reminder of the price of their ill-fated ambush.

Drak seething with rage as he rose from the ground where he was seated, sending out a shockwave of energy that rippled through the air as he unleashed an ear-splitting scream at Auorak, filling the air with its intensity.

"Holy hell!!! What did you do this for?! It smelled worse than an ogre when he had not bathed in weeks!" His muscles bulged and strained against his armor as he grabbed his war hammer to bash one of the remaining kobolds. "I think I'm going to be sick! UGHH! UGGH!" The stench overcame Drak as he deposited the contents of his stomach upon the ground.

Drak leaped to the ground and rolled left, narrowly dodging a kobold that had been sent flying by a massive blow from Barnabiz's war maul. The huge ogre continued, wildly swinging his maul like a grim reaper swinging its sky, the while singing a dirge about a busty bar wench. "There was a young lass from Berkenstein! Her name was Maggie MaeO'hary, and she was oh so damn scary!" And with a swift, downward swing, the massive maul took out another duo of unexpecting kobolds.

Blood and kobold innards flew through the air like soap bubbles caught in the wind as they seemed to burst against incorporeal creatures. The party was completely covered in blood and kobold viscera at this point, and their armor was caked in it from head to toe. Shrapnel from the exploding organs flew through the air and landed on everything visible.

Lupine, dropping from a low-hanging branch, rushed to the aid of his companions, piercing the throat of a kobold with a dagger as he tackled it to the ground. Blood splattered on its face and chest, and its screams were cut short by Lupine's second strike, which left only his dagger hilt protruding from the wretched little beast's eye socket. It twitched once, then fell lifeless.

"Holy shit! These little bastards reek! Are you sure they did not climb out from the ogre's asshole?" But none could argue as the kobolds did indeed have a unique odor. The stench was overwhelming, smelling of festering meat mixed with rancid sweat and mold.

The small creatures were ruthless and were cutting a swath through the party's ranks as if they had been trained for war. The warriors kept fighting on, each blow slashing kobold flesh to ribbons and spraying blood across the battlefield like an artist's brush painting with bright red fog. It was clear from their positions that the kobolds were only there to stall the party, perhaps even just to slow them down so other kobolds could ambush them.

But the party would not allow some terrified, scaly, miniature lizard men to stand in their way. What drove these little creatures to throw themselves at a band of seasoned warriors such as ours? Warriors whom they knew could kill them with sword, sorcery and sheer force of will.

After what felt like hours and hours of skirmishing, the party had finally dispatched all the kobolds; the only thing worrying them was the fact they were attacked by them at all. These little cowardly creatures never did anything of this sort. There was no real ambush or anything. Kobolds rarely attacked unless it was an ambush or the odds, so in their favor, the chance of loss was near nothing.

"Seventeen...seventeen? Only seventeen? I swear it was like there were at least fifty of those little, bow-legged scaly fuckers. They swarmed around us like bees in that beehive Barnabiz knocked down last year," explained Drak as the party accessed the carnage of battle. "It truly did look like there had been a massacre. And by the Lord of Light, it looks like we slaughtered a village."

It was true. Only seventeen kobolds lost their lives. There were well over one hundred originally. Drak was not imagining the sheer number of the cowardly little creatures. They had detected a much more dangerous foe, prompting them to retreat into the safety of the forest and their burrows. Or they were possibly fleeing from the greater threat all along, and our band of travelers were merely on the escape path.

The group was reeling from the battle with the kobolds, and they all had a giddy, almost drunken feeling as adrenaline coursed through their veins. A wicked storm had rolled in and started to rage as soon as they prepared to relax around the fire after such arduous fighting. Lightning and thunder clashed across the sky in flashes bright enough to blind most creatures. The wind had picked up, and debris swirled around the camp like a whirlpool.

Suddenly, two massive bugbears charged into camp, poised to attack Barnabiz, who was standing against a tree playing his lute in the rain and totally unaware of the intruders. The adventurers leaped to their feet to face the threat, but one of the giant bugbears lunged forward before they could get close. It swung its massive, misshapen club downward at Barnabiz as he managed to keep just out of range and kept singing, seemingly undaunted by the danger creeping closer.

The Bugbears

Leaping off of Navine's back, Nephrym dove into the air and plunged both of his daggers deep into the shoulders of the bugbear. His war cry echoed throughout the clearing as he mounted it like a horse and tamed it with his cold steel, driving his daggers ever deeper. At the same time, a raging bolt of eldritch fire shattered through the stomach of the other bugbear, incinerating its insides and knocking it to the ground. Lupine sprinted towards it with preternatural agility and drove his dagger straight into its spine. In an instant, the massive beast stopped moving as the last bits of life left its body.

Meanwhile, Drak made a beeline for the other bugbear and slammed his war hammer into its stomach with a single blow, shattering its bones and organs in an eruption of gore.

Navine quickly checked on Barnabiz while Nephrym tried to

perform an acrobatic dismount from the bugbear's back. Cursing at Drak for almost killing him. They all held up four fingers as Nephrym landed on the ground beside the now-dead beast.

"Hey, you could have fricking killed me!" Nephrym yelled, so agitated that he had almost destroyed himself.

"I had a good two feet of bugbear between my war hammer and your wee little feet!" Drak guffawed as he polished the monster's innards off his beloved weapon. "Am I losing my aim? You need to lay off the halfling's tobacco, and I think it is starting to make you a little loopy."

"Yeah, yeah. I don't know what you are talking about. My landing was at least an eight, maybe a nine or even higher," Nephrym said contemptuously as he passed by Barnabiz and Lupine. He wanted to show off a bit, but deep inside, he was conflicted. Part of him wanted to impress them, while the other part just wanted to curl up in a little ball and scream.

After almost an hour, the storm had finally given way to a relatively clear sky. Moving out almost as quickly as it had rolled in. The distant howling of wolves could now be heard off to the north and a band of coyotes off to the northwest. The occasional hooting of a great owl and the sound of whippoorwills permeated this unsettling night. Among the wind and heat of battle, someone had entered their camp and was sitting by the fire. The fire somehow did not go out in the torrential rain and gusting wind. It was sitting on a log by the fire, dressed in a bright neon blue bunny suit and holding a metallic staff. And not any type of neon blue, a sparkling neon blue. Its hair messily sticking out everywhere around the face.

Ever so quietly, watching the campfire, seemingly fascinated with the flames as they flickered and danced about. It was faintly whispering, "Burn, burn, burn, burn" to itself. Just loud enough for everyone to hear.

The Crazy Satyr

"What in the gnome's bloody boots do we have here?" asked Barnabiz as he looked over at the rest of the party. "You all see this, too, right? One of those bugbears punched me in the eye! Oh, wait a minute. I didn't get hit or anything. Right? Guys? What's going on here? I remember... something about this weirdo from somewhere. This is getting really weird again. Fuck!"

"Hell, I'm not sure what it was exactly. But from the looks and sound of it, I'd say batshit crazy with a side of kill the shit out of it fits the bill quite nicely," stated Lupine as he slowly flanked the creature, trying to get a closer look at it.

"Kill it?" he proposed.

"You dare to call someone batshit crazy? You, an unnatural, thieving creature of darkness, whose only answer is to kill everything, enemy or not, without a second thought?" Nephrym sneered as he slowly paced around the unknown figure, giving him no chance of escape.

"Who are you, and why are you in our camp?" Navine's thunderous voice boomed as she stepped forward with her drawn sword held tightly in her grasp.

"Be quick with your response or suffer dearly at the hands of my comrades. I advise you to speak, for you have no idea what depraved acts they may do unto you," she commanded, her menacing gaze fixed on the cowering figure.

He jumped into the air and spun around. The group noticed that he had cloven hooves and looked a bit like a satyr, but he was dressed in a blue bunny costume. A radiantly electric blue bunny costume, to be exact.

"My name is Sun Blast, the Ever Knowing. Nice to meet you all," the strange creature extended his hand toward Navine as he spoke.

Don't touch it! It could be carrying some type of disease, "Drak cut in before Navine could touch it, smacking her hand away from the mysterious creature. He breathed a silent sigh of relief; he was thankful he didn't have to cure everyone again, like when they got a surprise from a certain tavern wench, or that time they all caught leprosy, or the incident with the crypt rot... But those stories could wait for another day.

Nephrym and Lupine stalked silently up from behind, eyes blazing with animalistic fury. Even though there was an aura of dread in the air, Nephrym snarled a laugh and called out, Don't worry. I do not think bat shit crazy is contagious - otherwise, we'd all have it by now." Both of them remained tense as they prepared to pounce at any second, ready to unleash a punishing backstab at any sign of trouble.

Barnabiz sneered as he inspected the tiny creature that had intruded on his camp. "What do you think you're doing here?" he growled. A sickly, sweet, foul smell wafted off the creature, and Barnabiz recoiled disgustingly. His lips curled in disdain as he snarled, "You reek! I vote we drown it in the river we passed before dusk. At least then it will be bathed when it meets whatever gods it answers to."

"I am in hiding. I am stuck in this form. I am a dragon. An ancient gold dragon. People are hunting for me because of my lucky charms, which are just my treasure. And my gold. Most definitely after my gold. Oh, did I tell you I was a dragon? A gold dragon, to be exact. And no one tells you about the shit when you're really, really old and really, really rich. Come take a load off, and let me tell you about it... SHHHH...now if I could only remember where in the fuck, I put it," chuckled the odd little creature as he burst into a fit of dance around the fire. He danced around the campfire three times while singing, "The redcoats are coming! The redcoats are coming! Run for your lives! The redcoats are coming!" as he darted back into the forest and the brush.

"Seriously, you guys all saw what happened, right?" asked Drak as he slowly turned and visually inspected the camp. "Now that was some seriously messed up shit there, my friends."

"No more! Not a single puff of this foul, halfling weed. I warned you it smelled suspicious. We're done for! The tiny rascal has done us in with his nasty bud." Nephrym flung off his bag and urgently searched through the pouch an acquaintance from the Halfling Clan weeks back had given him.

"Let us not get too hasty, my minuscule, little friend. I have a feeling that before all of this is over, we will all need a drag from that halfling pipe of yours," sighed Drak as he took in all the things that had happened in such a short time. Barely made it past the first couple of days and already had two attempts on their lives and had a run-in with the crazy, whatever the hell that was.

"Seriously, you guys, we need to figure out what is going on here. First, a band of kobolds is nowhere near anything they could call home. And they boldly attacked us with no ambush or anything. And face it, there was something not right about those bugbears. We won too easily." Navine paced back and forth over the two giant corpses. Today had been full of oddities, but this went way beyond strange. Two bugbears, out alone and marching into our camp outnumbered? Something was not right, and the entire group knew it.

The howling of the wolves was now growing much louder as the sky above them cleared, revealing a blood-red moon. Despite the eerie nature of the sight, everyone was strangely entranced. It was one of the eeriest and yet most beautiful sights to behold.

"Tis a blood moon tonight, my fellow adventure junkies. Death is out and about," Barnabiz said in a solemn voice before beginning to sing a dirge about the god of death and killing in the crimson moonlight. A loud crack of thunder suddenly broke the beauty and darkness of the moment, and all heads turned to see a figure in the shadows, shrouded in the darkness of the forest.

From the south, the party heard a wolf pack's distant, sometimes angry, and sometimes sad call. The weak crimson light filtering through the clouds turned the thick woods an ominous red. The lone figure made its way into the camp. Gods only knew what sort of hellish beast this was. Navine was in no mood to find out and drew her battle mace, stepped forward, and spoke loudly, "Who is there?"

What she saw looked like a man covered in blood and fresh claw marks, muscular and seemingly stark naked with blood running down his body and splattered upon his face, almost as if he had bathed in it. From head to toe, he was covered in it. His own arms were covered in jagged wounds where claws had raked him. His body was covered in bits of bloody meat and chunks of bone fragments. In addition, his whole body was still dripping with blood from what appeared to have been attacked by some monstrous animal.

A bewildered look crossed his features, and he said over and over, "I killed them all, I killed them all."

Over and over, he repeated those words again and again. The young man fell backward over a log close to the fire, narrowly avoiding falling into the smoldering embers.

Laying stark naked by the fire had to be one of the largest humans any of them had ever seen.

"Seriously? Mage, if you're fucking with our heads, I swear I will smash your head like a grape with my war hammer!" remarked Drak boldly as he looked over at Auorak.

Giving him a look that could peel the bark from a tree. But Drak knew from the bewildered look upon Auorak's face this was none of his handy work.

"I swear, I've never messed with anyone's mind. Well, not really," Auorak declared as the entire party surrounded the human youth on the ground.

"What happened to you lad?" Navine asked, bending down to help him sit up straight. The paladin noticed the suffering and pain in his eyes as they locked onto hers. It was like staring into two burning pits of hellfire that could see inside her soul.

"Wait! What did you do one time!? I knew it!" Drak spat out, his eyes narrowing in accusation as he glared at Auorak.

"And look at him, lad! He's gigantic! Seven fucking feet tall and looks to be a teenager still. No 'lad'here - he is far more than that," his words thundered with anger and resentment, menacingly echoing off the walls.

"Ladies, hello? Definitely not the time. Hello, large, completely naked, and crazy boy in the camp!" Lupine yelled as he flanked the young lad.

"No, no. Let's get straight to it. Who the fuck are ya? And WHAT the hell are ya doing in our camp? And NAKED?" asked Barnabiz as he pushed Navine out of the way.

"Out of the way." Drak stepped around Barnabiz and kneeled beside the boy. The stiff, hard hands of a man accustomed to wielding a sword trembled gently over the boy's head, healing him and easing the eliciting moans of pain. He appeared much younger than Drak had first thought. He was indeed a teen, if not a boy. "What is your name, young lad? What in the god's name brings you to be wandering around naked and alone in the forest in this shape?"

"My name is Val'Rak. Please... help me. Please," the young boy sobbed. "I could not help it. I tried, but I could not help it. I lost control. I lost control and killed them all. I killed them all. Every last single one of them. You must believe me; I did not want to kill anyone. I could not stop. They kept on coming at me...I could not control myself and all the blood. I could not stop. The blood tasted so good I had to have more. And the feel of their flesh as it slid as I tore it from their bones...I could not control it," the boy was still pretty rushed up.

"Calm down. Tell me, who or what did this to you? What was the reason behind it? Were you being threatened? And who or what did you kill?" Drak questioned, attempting to be understanding and sympathetic as he spoke to the young man.

"It matters not. My sire and brothers, with their brutes, pursue me now. They will slay me, for I cannot become what Milord, my dad, desires. I have failed everyone," Val'Rak's sobs echoed in the night air.

Drak and Barnabiz stood above him, both of them scowling down at the boy. Aghast and appalled at his terrible situation. It was true, after all; he had been forsaken by his family and hunted like a wild beast.

What an appalling fate! Even the meanest creatures in hell wouldn't create such a tragedy. Our brave adventurers couldn't leave this young person to die. But inside each of them was a deep sadness because they had lost their childhood and had to grow up too fast, taking lives instead. Maybe, just maybe, they could save Val'Rak from the same fate.

"We must help him; no one can fault us for that! Just look at him sobbing and begging us for assistance. We can't turn away from this!" Navine implored the party, trying to convince them to aid the lad.

He's right...open your eyes and look at him. He may be a young boy, but he's larger than most men I know and probably stronger, too. And I am an ogre. Something is not right here. This whole situation makes my skin crawl. As I see it, we must rid ourselves of this before someone gets hurt. And that someone will be us!" Barnabiz observed as he paraded back and forth across the small camp, his boots tramping through the dead weeds and down onto the hard-packed dirt with each stride as he was smashing the route of his problems into the ground in the hopes that it would go away.

"And he keeps going on about having killed a bunch of people," reminded Lupine as the party tried to decide what the best course of action was. "We are far from a bunch. Hell, we are barely a gathering?"

Suddenly, a high-pitched shriek screamed through the air. In the moment it took for the sound to echo across the vast plain, Val'Rak doubled over in what looked like unbearable pain. Whatever he had just experienced had caused him severe pain and anguish but had passed for now.

"What in the hell happened? What exactly did your family do to you?" questioned Drak as he helped the boy sit back up again. "My family did not do anything to me. I was born this way. It is simply who I am. I must learn to control it," Val'Rak sobbed as he seemingly pleaded to the party. "Please, please do not hurt me."

"Exactly what do you have to learn to control? You are not some freaky ass spell chucker, are you?" inquired Lupine as he slowly backed away from the young boy.

"You guys have all seen what uncontrolled wild magic can do to you. Remember the goblin we met? The one who got hit by it never was the same. And remember how he looked? Holy hell, was he messed up."

"I believe him. I can tell he does not mean us any harm. He needs our help." Nephrym walked toward the boy. Gently placing his hand upon the lad's blood-flecked cheek, Nephrym said, "I truly believe he means us no harm whatsoever." Before another word could be uttered, a powerful and almost primal feeling overwhelmed Nephrym. His eyes locked onto the young person, who looked at him with such innocent longing and sadness that Nephrym could barely breathe around it. He felt ill at ease yet strangely comforted by this strange feeling of longing vulnerability. It was at that moment that the demon first ventured into Nephrym's mind.

The cloud covered parts suddenly, revealing the massive blood moon in all its magnificent glory. Its fiery crimson hue cast a ghastly glow over Val'Rak's body as he begins to thrash about wildly, convulsing and screaming in agony. The party watched in stunned awe as the boy's limbs twisted and contorted, his muscles bulging unnaturally beneath his skin.

With each passing moment, his face is becoming more bestial, his teeth sharpened into dagger-like points, and claws sprouting from each of his fingertips with an audible crack. The very air around him rippled and twisted like a reflection in disturbed water, with each violent thrash becoming more bestial.

"Gods preserve us!" Nephrym cried in terror, stumbling back from the abomination that was before them. Val'Rak had grown to heights of unearthly proportions, standing upon two horrifically transformed legs and crowned with a great mass of savage fur.

The beast had grown a monstrous set of claws and teeth, which glinted maliciously in the pale crimson light of the blood moon. It could not be mistaken; this thing was no mere werewolf but an incarnation of all the evils that dwelled beneath the night sky. The group felt a chill settle upon them as they now fully understood the magnitude of their foe.

Val'Rak

"Hello, gentlemen, and cow! I am hungry...so ravenous. I can almost feel my stomach growling in anticipation!" growled Val'Rak as he stared directly into Nephrym's eyes.

"Holy shit! It talks! They are not supposed to talk!" screamed Drak as he pulled out his Warhammer. "I have battled many beasts of the moon, and none of them have ever talked!"

"I have never tasted gnome before...and you smell absolutely delicious!" Val'Rak lunged towards Nephrym in one leap, landing on top of him and pinning him to the ground. His great weight crushed the air from his lungs, and Nephrym struggled for a moment not to suffocate under the tough, fur-covered body.

Barnabiz swung his massive maul at the beast. The heavy spiked-iron ball of the weapon hit with a dull thud, taking the creature's breath away and knocking the beast off of Nephrym, landing a few feet away. Val'Rak leaped to his feet and readied himself. He looked around to get his bearings as he tasted the metallic tang of blood in his mouth. A wolfish howl shook him from his stupor and snapped him back into focus on what was important.

"Great! A fucking werewolf! The kid is a fucking werewolf!" Nephrym screamed as he drew his daggers and readied to strike Val'Rak.

"Destroy him!" roared Auorak as he set off a powerful blast of eldritch fire. Brilliant tongues of flame illuminated the campsite and crackled forth from his fingers, though barely enough to scorch Val'Rak's coarse fur. Looking around at his companions in bewilderment, Auorak exclaimed, "What the hell? Is he immune to magic?"

"Give me the gnome or suffer for your insolence! You dare attack me?" boomed Val'Rak as he flew towards Nephrym, who could only cower in fear, feeling as if his very life was hanging by a thread. "Who are we kidding? You all die here tonight."

"Since when do you dogs speak?" Still amazed that he had never heard tales of one which could. "And as for you getting the gnome? Not happening, mutt!" Drak watched as Val'Rak shrugged off the blow to the side of his head and charged him with a howl.

"Nephrym! Climb up!" shouted Navine as she positioned herself between Nephrym and Val'Rak. All of a sudden, loud howls could be heard in the distance off in the east. Val'Rak stopped, and an entirely different look replaced the once ferocious maw. A look of concern and fear at the same time. Val'Rak turned and started to run towards the distant howls.

He stopped for a brief second and turned toward Nephrym. "I will not let them have you! They can never have you! I will lead them away from you, my confidante. You belong to me!" Tears appeared to be welling up in the beast's eyes.

"What the hell is this? Do you think gnomes are some sort of tasty werewolf treat?" Drak spat out, his eyes boring holes into Nephrym's as he asked the question. His face contorted into a mask of intrigue and disgust.

"Gnome is tough, chewy and gamey. Not for everyone. Best when paired with a heavy, robust gravy, stout ale, and slow-roasted with lots of herbs and root vegetables to bring out the earthiness. Takes lots of practice to perfect," Barnabiz explained as he wiped his maul off. "Old ogre delicacy."

The rest of the party sort of stares at Barnabiz for a brief second. They were all clearly shocked and disgusted by his previous statement, but only for a moment. "What? Times were hard!" Barnabiz laughed.

"And like I said, old ogre delicacy."

"Go ahead! Try to eat me. I dare you! I will give your stank, ogre-ass indigestion for at least a decade," Nephrym replied.

The rest of the night passed in relative quiet, excluding the snide comments and rude gestures. No one was very surprised. They, after all, were all part of this motley party. The party awoke to yet another day of adventure as the sun broke through the clouds. As grateful as they were for the peaceful hours of sleep, they looked forward to what the day ahead would bring even more.

"Who knew the feel of sunshine could be so good?" Lupine remarked as he fastened his armor and picked up his gear. A three-day journey, if they didn't run into trouble, to the cottage of the man who hopefully knew something about what was going on.

Barnabiz rubbed his shoulder, where a bandage held in place by a fresh salve that covered a fresh wound from some of his recent battles — which one, he had no idea. They had been lucky this time. Maybe they would have one night without worrying about strange magic, bugbears, or werewolves.

Chapter 2
We Came Here For This/Oh Look A Peep Show

They continued, every step taking them farther away from the sounds of civilization and closer to meeting whatever it was the gods had in store for them. Only they knew what truly awaited. After three days of uneventful travel, they happened upon a cottage nestled in a nook between two hills.

A cottage, according to the map given to them by Reto, should be his mentor's Retsnimle house. They hoped that he could shed some light on the current situation.

"I thought Reto said his mentor was a gnome, like Nephrym?" Drak asked as he surveyed the cottage. "Why in the hell would a gnome live in a place like this? I mean, look at the doors!"

"I don't like it. Something about this whole place is creepy to me," Nephrym remarked as he veered down from his usual perch on Navine's pack. As the dirt and stone path beneath their feet gave way to the cool grass of the clearing, a small gnome dressed in flowing black robes trimmed in crimson stepped out of the cottage door and signaled them forward.

The back of the robe was so deep it absorbed the light around it and made him appear smaller and somehow less threatening. The crimson trim looked like it was flowing, like rivers of blood if you stared at them long enough.

"A simple observation, if you will... why does a two-foot-tall gnome need eight-foot doors? Anyone? Bit off, perhaps?" questioned Nephrym as they followed the gnome inside. "I mean, I am a gnome, and I do not have eight-foot doors at my place."

"Retsnimle's the name. Make yourself comfortable. We have lots to discuss. I hope your journey here was not too boring." Chuckled Retsnimle as he motioned everyone to follow him and he sat down in an ornately carved rocking chair by the fireplace. "And my pint-sized friend, I have eight-foot-tall doors and ten-foot-tall ceilings for such occasions as this," he looked at Nephrym with that remark.

"So, you regularly have large ogres in your living room?" questioned Lupine as he surveyed the room. All the while thinking what wonders there must be to thief in this place. The things that he could steal if only given the time. "I'd be careful. I think our ogre secretly has a taste for gnome flesh. We are trying to break him, though," he added.

"Why, I have all sorts of visitors, and I strive to give them only the best accommodation and whatever they desire," smiled Retsnimle. "No one likes a bad host, now, do they?" He said while giving Nephrym a disgruntled look that would rival the stare of a Medusa.

"Ok. We are here like Reto asked of us. Now what?" Auorak said as he approached the chair the old gnome mage was sitting in. His attention to detail was automatically drawn to the small, white flower that sat on top of a nearby table, and he immediately brought his hand up to smell it, only to find that it was not there. Old, dark, and mysterious magic felt unfamiliar and unsettling to someone as skilled as Auorak.

"Reto and I had an undertaking of sorts, a quest if you will. A quest of the utmost importance. One much needs to be completed. The existence of the Land of Dodd as we know it may well be in the maiden's balance Obviously, by him sending you, whom he spoke highly of most of the time, he felt as I do," Retsnimle stated as he started to rock back and forth in the rocking chair.

"There are some ancient Elven ruins which lay roughly three weeks travel to the northeast. Less if you're not afraid of portals. Your journey will first lead you there. These ruins are heavily protected by various types of beasts, traps, and all sorts of long-forgotten magics. Nothing a skilled group like yourselves should be concerned about, I'm sure. In these ruins, there is a treasure beyond your wildest dream. I care nothing of treasure. You can keep all you find. Just save a few items I need to procure. They are items long since forgotten by almost everyone. By most beings of our world anyway. If their power should become known to the wrong people, the end of our world as we know it would be upon us," he said, his voice lowering to a grave whisper as a shadow crossed his face.

"What exactly are these items? And what in the nine hells make you think we can procure them?" Auorak asks. "If these items hold as much power as you say, there must be others searching for them or have and failed to find them."

The old gnome said, "I see more than you will ever know. There are many forces at war with one another as we stride forward from this point. Your destinies lie within those walls. In life or death, we cannot ignore our destiny. It is written by the Gods and Goddesses long before we are brought into existence. I will send you a message when you get to the ruins. You and your friends simply knowing of their existence at this point is a danger to you all."

Then, the old gnome walked over and handed Nephrym a map before walking back to the table and picking up his small pack with only a few items in it. He opened the door to reveal what most would call the kitchen of his cottage.

"I must go now. I have a few errands which I must take care of and simply cannot wait any longer. You have a map that will lead you to the Elven ruins. Feel free to take whatever supplies you need from my cellar. There is a village about four days' travel from here called Wolfsven. It is on the route you must take. Go to the general store and talk to a human man named Svenly. Let him know you work for me. I will have arranged for you to procure any needed supplies which I do not have." Looking over at Nephrym, he said, "I see that your tastes are a bit more exotic in nature. Perhaps I can help you out with that as well." He laughed as he walked out the door and vanished into thin air.

"I don't like the creepy little fucker," Nephrym said as he looked out the door. "Something about him makes my skin crawl."

The thought of the creepy old mage making sexual remarks toward him made his stomach twist and rumble. "The way he looks at me makes me feel dirty inside," Nephrym said with an ick.

"You're a creepy little fucker as well, ya know?" said Barnabiz as he sat down in front of the fireplace.

"Screw you! You, big ogre bastard!" laughed Nephrym as he came back inside, shutting the door behind him.

"I think the little man was right. You do have exotic tastes, my little gnome friend. Never knew it was sausages and tube steak," Barnabiz laughed as he started belting out a bawdy tale about a young man being molested by an orcish horde. Leave it to Barnabiz to not only breach the door to illicit behavior but crash through it like a drunken troll into a campsite.

"Seriously? Fucking ogre lunker! Don't think I do not know who you are referring to. Not now, not tomorrow, but someday, I am going to get you. And when I do, it is going to be epic," sighed Nephrym in disgust as he sat down beside the fire and relaxed with an ale in hand. "I had almost forgotten what ale tasted like. Almost," he said with a wistful smile, savoring the moment as the warmth of the drink spread through him.

"It has only been a bit over two weeks since we started this godforsaken journey. You all act as if we have not drank or eaten the entire time," laughed Auorak as he enjoyed a portion of boar.

"I know, it has been absolute hell, has it not?" asked Lupine in agreement with Nephrym.

"You would think you two little bastards were dwarves as much as you drink!" Drak chuckled as he slammed back a tankard of Retsnimle's homemade ale.

"Says the half-dragon who finished up what his fourth or fifth tankard of ale?" asked Lupine as he poured yet another for Nephrym and himself.

"Seventh, to be exact. We dragon-born can hold our liquor. Besides, I am part dwarven three times removed on my father's side," bellowed Drak as he slammed yet another bottle of ale.

After devouring a nourishing meal and copious amounts of ale, the adventurers decided to take advantage of the mage's hospitality and get some much-needed rest. To everyone's surprise, the cottage was far larger within than without due to its magical properties.

Every member of the party finds their own private bedroom with a warm bath and the chance to repair their blood-mired and worn gear. After spending so long only snatching occasional naps between encounters on the trip, everyone slipped into a deep sleep.

Suddenly, Barnabiz was startled from his sleep by a commotion coming from the main room downstairs. He raced down as quickly as he could, naked as the day he was born, to investigate the source of the disturbance. But if the sight of an enormous naked ogre wielding an immense maul is not shocking enough, his eyes were met with something else entirely: a mysterious figure seated in the rocking chair beside the fireplace. It was none other than the young werewolf lad they had encountered in the forest. It was Val'Rak. It was Val'Rak and Nephrym.

Val'Rak's eyes were wild, eerie, and unearthly as they flashed in the dim light. Nephrym lay limp in the young werewolf lad's grip, and Barnabiz knew that he should step in, but something held him back. Deep down, he felt he had to do something. That he should stop whatever was happening. But for whatever reasons he could not understand, he just could not.

"Threaten to get me, you little bugger. Now you're the one getting buggered," Barnabiz grinned to himself as he watched Val'Rak's restless movements, savoring the moment until a clamor of voices made its way to where he stood.

With a single movement, Barnabiz whipped up his arm and blocked Drak, Lupine, Auorak, and Navine from advancing any farther, lest they disrupt whatever was actually going on here.

"Let's not be hasty. Nephrym is not getting hurt. I think he and the wolf boy got shit-faced together after we went to bed, and now they are about to throw down. And by throw down, I mean shit is about to get weird, so to speak," Barnabiz told the rest of the party as what appeared to be Nephrym's trousers flew over their heads. Val'Rak threw them.

"My bad," Baranbiz said as he watched the two in the rocking chair.

"Shit has already gotten weird. They are getting down. No doubt about it. Fucking hell!" Barnabiz laughed and reached and grabbed a bottle of what he hoped was ale someone had left out to take a drink.

"I do not know about all of this," Drak said, a worried tone in his voice.

"Are they doing what I think they are doing? Is Nephrym being hurt?" he was truly concerned.

Barnabiz didn't respond at first, letting the two proceed with their dance of depravity, undisturbed by their audience.

"If he was raping him, Nephrym would be putting up a fight. We would have heard something," remarked Barnabiz. "Besides, looks to me as if the little gnome bastard is having quite the time."

"Besides, from the look on his face and the drool running down his chin, I think he is rather enjoying himself. Enjoying himself a bunch," he smirked.

"I am not so sure it is drool," Lupine said as he paled and vomited a little in his mouth.

"Leave it to the goblin and the ogre to go there," Navine remarked in disgust. "Filthy pigs, all of you," he commented.

A loud sound of fabric filled the chamber as clothes were torn off and flew through the air. Soon, Val'Rak and Nephrym sat in the rocking chair nude, lit only by a bright fire that crackled in the fireplace. The other guests watched with bated breath, their eyes wide with fascination and fear. It was like two grotesque mannequins had come to life, their bodies moving awkwardly together to some music of love that no one could hear. A sensual scene of intimate gothic horror that no one would soon forget and would forever be etched into their memories.

"Hey, from my experience. If you're fucking, you're drooling, and your eyes are rolled back in your head. It is not rape. It's a fricking party," laughed Barnabiz as he sat down. Fully intending to see this show to fruition, "Besides, if wolfy lad starts to get fuzzy and starts taking the gnome to pound town, we will step in and stop it. But only if it gets out of hand. Are we clear? Besides, this is one of the best shows I've ever seen. You know what a show like this would cost?"

An arrow whistled through the air, a deathly shriek of metal aimed straight at its victim. It sank deep into the back of the rocking chair with a sickening crunch, sending splinters of wood flying in all directions.

"There, you saw it. I tried to stop it. I tried," Lupine muttered, his voice choking with horror and disbelief. "HOLY HELL! The lad is packing some heat there. His little gnome ass will be able to shit square and not feel a damn thing after this."

He can't take his eyes off what is taking place in front of him, trapped in a moment of utter terror and despair. Conflicted on whether or not he should feel good or bad for his friend.

"Question if I might inquire. He is a werewolf. Nephrym is a gnome. Does this mean he is into bestiality? I mean don't get me wrong, Navine is hot as hell for a minotaur and all, but she isn't really my type. I always thought the Nephrym seemed to have a thing for her," laughed Drak as he still stood there with everyone in disbelief, trying to process what he was seeing. Thinking this must be a dream he was going to wake from at any time.

"Holy shit!" he said out loud, his jaw-dropping opened and his eyes glued to the scene unfolding before him. He couldn't believe what he was watching nor the fact that he was witnessing it unfurl, entirely enthralled by it. Young Val'Rak shifted into his werewolf form in what seemed like an instant.

Val'Rak scooped Nephrym up in one powerful arm and cradled him gently. The werewolf lad began licking the gnome all over, tenderly running his tongue from head to toe. Nephrym's eyes closed as he enjoyed the soothing sensation of Val'Rak's rough tongue, and a look of pleasure passed between them.

"Ok...now this is some fucked up shit right there. First, he fucked the gnome's ass; now, he licked the gnome clean. Must be some sick werewolf shit there?" Barnabiz said as he got up. "I am an ogre, and I draw the line at felching."

"Hey, he is a dog, you know," laughed Lupine as he turned around. Now bored of the whole escapade and still exhausted. "I'm going back to sleep. So, the gnome is going to have a sore ass for a day or two. I tried to intervene. You all saw it. I tried, I really did."

"Day or two, hell, the little bastard is not ever going to walk right again!" laughed Barnabiz.

"We can always have the paladin lay on hands and heal him." Auorak laughed.

"She got grossed out or pissed off a few minutes ago and left," Drak said. "I don't know if she and the gnome had something going on and she was jealous. But after seeing him naked, unless he was crawling up in that thing and doing jumping jacks, it's hard to see how she could have been getting any pleasure from that," Drak laughed as he decided it was time to retire once again for the night.

Val'Rak tenderly dressed Nephrym, his fingers traced reverently over the gnome's skin as if he was a priceless work of art. He laid him down on an ornate rocking chair that creaked gently under his weight and covered him with a thick fur blanket. But as he tucked Nephrym in, his mind raced with anxiety, for he knew what must come next.

Convincing his father that Nephrym was not just another conquest. As a sixteen-year-old prince of one of the largest werewolf packs in the realm, Val'Rak had slept with more than half of the pack members his age, both male and female. But Nephrym was different.

Val'Rak longed to introduce him to the ways of the pack and make him undergo the ritual that would transform him into a true member of their family.

Only then could they return home and show Nephrym the inner workings of their society. Nephrym had no clue what lay ahead of him, the good and the bad, that could shape him forever. He became heir to one of the wealthiest families in all the realms and led one of the most powerful political entities ever to grace Dodd's landscape — the House of Val.

On this fateful night, many wheels had been set in motion, forces that had left indelible scars upon the Land of Dodd.

Nephrym

Chapter 3

The Morning After

As the sun cascaded through the windows, a thick tension filled the air. No one wanted to be the first to address the night before when Val'Rak had swooped in unannounced and had his way with the petite gnome as if he were some bandit escaping with a bag of gold.

Nephrym finally came stumbling out of his room with an aura of energy that only confirmed what everyone was thinking — no one had any doubts about what had taken place between them the night before.

Barnabiz rolled his eyes and glared at the gnome; his head cocked to one side. "My, aren't we a bundle of fucking sunshine this morning?" he said through clenched teeth.

Drak raised his eyebrows and took a sip from his stein before letting out an incredulous laugh and spitting it back out in disgust, some of the ale splashing against a nearby wall. "All of the extra protein, huh?" he said, shaking his head.

"I slept well. What can I say?" remarked Nephrym as he poured up an ale for a good start at breakfast. The room buzzed with quiet amusement, but no one dared ask for more details. Hearing Nephrym, Drak again spat ale all over the floor as he and everyone else there except for Nephrym burst into laughter.

"What the fuck is so funny?" asked Nephrym as he sat down in the rocking chair by the fireplace. "You love the rocking chair, don't ya, little buddy? Brings back those fond memories of getting rocked to sleep?" laughed Barnabiz as he sat down and poured another flagon of ale.

"I do. I find it comfortable and relaxing at the same time. Give me a few ales, a warm fire, almost as good as sex." Nephrym replied as he started rocking back and forth. His short gnome legs were dangled not touching the floor.

"Looks like I need a stool," he said with a laugh while everyone remained curious but stayed silent.

Everyone at this point, except for Nephrym, was laughing to the point of tears almost. Barnabiz was laughing so hard he was doubled over, gasping for air.

"Let me tell him! Please let me tell him!" Barnabiz said as he literally rolled onto the floor. "Fucking please, I beg of you all."

"Nephrym, what do you remember about last night?" Lupine questioned as he approached the gnome. "We ate, had a few ales, and we all went to sleep. Why?" asked Nephrym, now puzzled and wondering what was going on.

"I think you might have had a little much to drink, pal. I came up to get a late nightcap and found you and the wolf lad from yesterday rutting around at each other like two rabid weasels in a ruck sac. Right there in that rocking chair." Lupine explained to Nephrym while trying hard to keep a straight face. "And the ogre was standing at the bottom of the stairs butt ass naked watching."

"Ha Ha...not fucking funny," smirked Nephrym in disbelief. "Because I manage actually to take advantage and sleep you want to poke fun? Go ahead, poke the gnome all you like. I feel amazing this morning. Best sleep I have ever had."

"Um...He's not joking," Navine said, her voice trembling with embarrassment for her friend. Her gaze shifted nervously between the others in the room before settling on Barnabiz. The look on her face said a lot, showing a mix of disgust and judgment.

"We all heard it and came out to watch, I mean, see what was going on." she continued, her words strained with emotion. "Some of us watched much more than others."

41

"Let's be perfectly honest here now, folks. Werewolf lad was up in you like a gopher in a hole. A deep hole. Cavernous deep hole." Barnabiz howled with laughter.

"Bullshit!" Nephrym shouted, his face twisted in disbelief. His hands shook at his sides, and he could feel the faint sting of pain radiating from his backside as the memories slowly returned to him. He didn't understand how he could have done something like this without any recollection, and yet he felt a strange sense of comfort come over him when he thought of Val'Rak, something that he'd never experienced before. A feeling that somehow made him feel whole and torn apart all at once.

"We have all overindulged ourselves at one point or another." Navine's voice was soft and regretful as she tried to give Nephrym comfort, wrapping her arms around him.

Nephrym groaned. "I am never drinking again," he said, his eyes opening wide as the wild night before came rushing back to him.

"We have all been there at one time or another! Granted, I have never been drunk to the point I hooked up with a teenage werewolf for a random sexcapade drunk," laughed Drak as he shook his head, a grin spreading across his face. "I think I understand why you and Navine have always been so close now. The two of you were talking about dudes, weren't you?"

"Enough already. So, the gnome got his backdoor canal rooted out. We got money to make. Let's gear up and get the hell out of here before the were lad comes back and decides he wants something other than the gnome." Aurok barked as he started to pack his gear up.

Over the next few hours, the party gathered up food, munitions and virtually anything that could be of use for their journey. Retsnimle had told them the ruins were about a few week's travel from his cottage. And they needed to stop in a small hamlet of Wolvenston for the rest of their supplies.

After packing the food and supplies that would be needed from Retsnimle's stores, the party decided to finally embark on the next leg of their journey. They could not help but wonder what was in store for them as they started this trek into the unknown.

The clouds drifted across the bright blue sky like churning gray flocks of sheep. It was about three hours after lunch when the party became suddenly aware of a carriage about a quarter of a mile or so up the road.

The Royal Carriage

The carriage traveled north with what appeared to be forty heavily armed soldiers on horseback and twelve elite Knights, who were all dressed like demons out of hell in gleaming red plate armor. The burning reddish mane and tail of the horses contrasted against their ebony bodies, seeming to burn like flames as they snorted and pawed at the ground. Their sharp hooves made a scuffling sound in the dirt as each struck down with meaty thuds.

All of the soldiers and knights had drawn swords, holding them high in two hands over their heads, ready to strike like snakes striking from under old logs. As they descended upon the unsuspecting travelers, they shouted out orders with deep voices that matched their appearance. Our group of friends froze in fear, realizing they were outnumbered and had little chance of escape. Suddenly, a wide set of powerful shoulders, enhanced by the delicate leather armor he wore beneath his shaggy coat, broadened as the man exited the carriage. Nearly nine feet tall and dressed in exquisitely detailed black leather armor with fighting wolves emblazoned upon it, this person was a vision of power and grace.

"Greetings, my good people. Please allow me to introduce myself. I am Lord Vladumir 'Val of the House of Val." His voice was heavy with emotion as he bowed before them. "I have a difficult request to make of you all, one which has been thrust upon me in an unfortunate turn of events. My son went missing last night, and after our search, we found him safe and sound thanks to a band of travelers in the forest. One which, from his description, is much like yourselves. He now wishes to travel with that party, against my wishes, so that he may experience things beyond our lands."

Lord Vladumir'Val

"Bloody fucking hell, the gnome's ass wolf has brought his daddy and his cronies to fucking kill us." Remarked Barnabiz to the rest of the party.

"I only hope they wanna kill us. And not rape us all to death!" said Lupine, chuckling as he realized he was laughing aloud.

"Why exactly would we want to let your son join us? The only person we helped was a young lad who turned out to be a werewolf and so happened to try and kill all of us. So please, explain to me why we would want the lunatic to join us?" Asked Drak as he tried to survey the situation. Seeing no alternative other than having to fight their way out of this situation. "This is a potential thorn in our side we can do without. We have work to be done. We have not time to be nursemaids for your pup."

"My son is very apologetic about most of what occurred last night. Please forgive him, for he was not himself. He had not yet completed his oath to our pack and was at the mercy of the blood moon's fury. He was not in full control of his actions. Now, he has completed and honored his oath to the pack and is in full control of his abilities. I reluctantly have decided to allow it if you agree. The connection he shares with the little gnome is one he assures me is a unique and special one. The blood moon blesses it as well. All I am asking is you give him a chance to join you. He is extremely capable of holding his own in combat. And I assure you he will by oath defend each of you with his life if allowed to join you. And I will gladly pay you a sum of five thousand gold coins. And upon the safe return of my son at the end of your journeys, another five thousand gold coins." The lord replied as he stood and stared at the party, paying particular attention to Nephrym.

"Look, guys. I get it," Lupine said, looking around at the rest of the group and the towering lord. " He wants to let his inner wolf run wild with its tongue hanging out of its mouth and just howl at the moon up in the starry sky. I mean, seriously, if Wolfenstein only wants to toss the gnome's salad. For ten thousand gold, I have no problem. No problem at all. Who am I to judge? I say let your freak flag fly. And if that means you have wild, drunken, young werewolf sex with a gnome, so be it," said Lupine, grinning as he crossed his arms and leaned against the carriage.

"Esteemed company, I implore you to consider my son, Val'Rak, in your ranks. He has mastered his abilities and is ready to embark on his journey of glory and honor as a noble adventurer. Your graciousness in this matter will be remembered and highly regarded. Help a doting father fulfill his son's dream. The crown will be in your debt."

"Oh, I think his dream came true last night. I am pretty sure someone came. Ask the gnome. He has been dripping from his ass all morning." Laughed Lupine as he turned to Nephrym and mimicked what he saw last night.

"It's a deal! Five thousand gold coins now, and five thousand when we bring the boy back safely in one year... assuming he can manage to stay alive. That goes without saying, right? He will be treated like every other in our group, but we will not babysit him. If he does something young and stupid and dies, we shall not be responsible." Auorak glared at his opponent with fierce determination.

"Deal." The gentleman shook Auorak's hand and proceeded back to the carriage. Va_'Rak stepped out of the carriage, wearing the same black leather armor as his father and brandishing two exquisite longswords.

"Thank you, thank you all. I promise you won't regret letting me join you on this adventure." Young Val'Rak stated as his father bade him farewell and boarded the carriage once more. The rattling of wheels on gravel as the horses lunged forward caused the carriage to barrel forward at a speed that was astounding for a horse and carriage. Disappearing in a whirlwind of dust, leaving the sound of hooves echoing in the air behind them.

And with a simple business transaction, all remaining normality has vanished. There was not anything normal about our misfit assortment of sorts. Hopefully, they will be the right sort of misfits to save the Land of Dodd. As of this moment, events have been set into motion which will hold dire consequences for the future of our great Land of Dodd. These events had been prophesized for millennia, and the bards will weave tales of them for millennia to come.

"Okay. Rule number one. The only ass you can sniff is the gnomes and only the gnomes. Rule number two. The only bunghole shenanigans you can or will embark on are with said gnome. All other assholes are strictly off-limits and forbidden. Is this clear?" Barnabiz said to Val'Rak as he walked around the lad, giving him a once over and hoping he could handle himself in battle at least enough to survive without a babysitter. "And you had better be able to use those pig stickers. Any nave can carry a blade. Let us see if you are man enough actually to wield them."

Nephrym's feet dragged as he walked over to Val. He tried his best to avoid the glares and snickers from the others. Tucking his hands deep in his pockets, Nephrym cleared his throat before speaking up.

"They are all messing with you, Val. Is it alright if I call you Val?" he said softly, unable to hide a hint of sorrow in his voice. His mind raced, questioning why he felt such an inexplicable connection to the young man in front of him. Not one for fleeting emotions, it puzzled him that something so foreign — something that defied logic — had taken root deep within him. There was just something about young Val that he knew that he could not say no to.

"Yes, please call me Val."

The adventuring party pressed onward toward their destination, yet an oppressive dread loomed over them, consuming the silence. The once unified group had been forced to confront a looming problem: they had not been trained to deal with a wild and restless, potentially dangerous teenager who just happened to be completely enamored with Nephrym and also cursed with lycanthropy.

Even more daunting was that he had possibly violated Nephrym in some way - rape, molestation, or something along those lines, or it could be love - and none of them knew how to react. Nothing but sheer fear of the unknown kept the peace and drove them onwards.

Drak twisted his lips into a sly smile as he rode up alongside Nephrym. "So...I gotta ask," he said, his voice laced with amusement. "You know the kid is only like sixteen, right? And you're like that seventy? You can get put in the stockade for the shit of this sort, you know." He paused for a moment, letting the words sink in before continuing. "And, since he is a werewolf, it's technically bestiality. You better stay in the paladin's good graces, or she might haul your little gnome ass in."

"How dare you?" Nephrym seethed, outraged. "I would expect this kind of behavior from the ogre or the goblin, but not you! I can feel my life spiraling away before my eyes as if I am a helpless puppet in some deranged show. Don't you understand what it feels like to have no control over your own fate?" He spat out his words, an invisible fire burning behind his pupils.

"No need to go getting all butthurt about it now. Oh wait, you probably are butthurt. I saw that shit go down. I have to say, I was impressed, and I'm an ogre. Wolf Boy is packing some serious heat.

Go, go, go, red rocket!" Barnabiz barely managed to get out as he was laughing so hard. He held up his hands in surrender as if warding off an attack.

Chapter 4
2 Rogues, One Brothel/This Town Has Gone To The Wolves

The bickering and bantering between the party members went on for what felt like an eternity. They traded insults and snide remarks, but to young Val'Rak's surprise, he came to realize that this was their way of accepting him into the group.

As the day wore on and the sun began to set, they finally reached the village of Wolfvenston. From afar, it looked like any other small hamlet with a few shops and taverns scattered about. But Val'Rak knew better - this was a lycanthrope sanctuary, a place where his father ruled as he did over all the Land of Dodd's lycanthropes with an unyielding iron fist.

The streets were lined with thick trees whose branches arched overhead, blotting out most of the sky. The air smelled of pine needles mixed with dirt and sweat. Houses made of wood dotted on either side of the cobblestone road leading through town. The occasional howl could be heard in the distance, harkening back to the lycanthrope origins of this sanctuary town. It was both awe-inspiring and terrifying.

"Well, isn't this a marvelous little shithole of a village?" Lupine remarked as he gave it to the old goblin once over. "Wonder how many guards they have, or better yet, where is the tavern?"

Val'Rak looked around at the small village of Wolfvenston, his eyes scanning over every detail. The buildings were crafted with care, each one unique in its own way. The streets were narrow and winding but clean and well-maintained. "Wolfvenston may be small," he said to the party, "but it is a hidden gem. They boast some of the best craftsmen in all of the Land of Dodd." He took out his coin purse and jingled it in his hand. "Let us all visit the bathhouse and relax for the evening. And then the tavern for a drink to heal sore muscles and bones." He couldn't risk being recognized on the streets any longer than necessary. Not a single soul in the group knew who he truly was, what he was, and Val'Rak intended to keep it that way for as long as possible. The longer he remained somewhat anonymous, the better off he would be.

Val'Rak

Young Val'Rak led the group to the local inn and procured a room for each of them. He was unsure whether to assume he and Nephrym would share a room or not. So, to be safe and not get any extra harassment from the party, he got separate rooms for both of them.

After taking a couple of hours to relax and unwind from their travels, the party made their way down to the public bath house, which so happened to serve as the local brothel. From the look on Nylissa's face as they approached and entered, she'd never seen such a strange group of people come through her doors.

"I am Lady Nylissa, and I have been expecting you. All of you." The tall, slim, elven lady glided from behind the counter to greet the party. A long white dress flowed around her like a cloud, catching in the soft, silky strands of her dark hair as it flowed out behind her. She was breathtakingly beautiful, almost regal, as she approached.

"And it got creepy." Lupine backed slowly away from the elven lady. "And how were you expecting us?"

"Why, Lord Reto stopped in and informed us that you would be here, of course." The elven woman smiled and sat down next to the goblin, stroking his chin. "I was told to take extra special care of you all," she said, her voice laced with a mix of amusement and mystery, "but Reto never warned me how charming you'd be."

Navine glanced uncertainly at the group of men, an uneasy feeling settling in her stomach.

"Okay then," she said hesitantly.

"I'll leave you to whatever is going on here. If any of you need healing, I'll be charging for it." She took a step back, ready to leave them and their strange business behind.

"I'll be at the temple if you need me," she finished before turning around and walking away. The lady paladin wanted no part of the assumed debauchery that was about to take place here.

Navine

"Please follow me, gentlemen. I have a room prepared for each of you." Nylissa walked down the long hallway, stopping at the first door.

"Barnabiz, if you will wait in here and disrobe. Someone will be with you shortly." Barnabiz gave the elven lady a grimacing look. There were few things in the entire Land of Dodd he hated more than elves. But that, alas, is a story for another day.

Still, her presence unnerved him. The way she smiled—so effortless, so infuriating—made his skin crawl. He shifted uncomfortably, resisting the urge to pull away from her touch.

"Care for me, eh?" he grumbled, his voice dripping with suspicion. "And what exactly did they promise you in return?"

The elven woman's smile didn't falter, though her eyes narrowed ever so slightly. "Promises mean little to me, ogre," she replied, her hand pausing beneath his chin. "But your fate... now that's something worth keeping an eye on."

Barnabiz stooped down, his leathery-skinned face mere inches from Val'Rak's. His low, raspy voice was just loud enough for the young man to hear. "What d'ya mean by disrobe?" Val snorted and shook his head as he leaned in conspiratorially. "It means take off all your clothes, you big oaf!" He winked cheekily at Barnabiz, who nodded knowingly before standing up with a grunt.

"Gentlemen, if you will." Nylissa walked down to the next door. "Lupine." And before she could say anymore, Lupine spurted out, "Go in, get naked and wait. Why yes, thank you."

Nylissa led the remaining party members to the next room. "Drak, specially prepared for you. Enjoy." She opened the door and walked down to the next one. "And young Lord Val'Rak and Nephrym, this room is yours. I believe the is much for you to discuss."

"We are sharing a room?" Nephrym's voice quivered as the reality of his situation hit him. Val'Rak stared into his eyes, scrutinizing his expression intently, before eventually responding in a calm yet stern voice: "Only if you want. I am not trying to force you to do anything you do not want. Are you sure this is what you want?" Overcome with emotion, Nephrym nodded helplessly as Val'Rak bent down and gently picked him up, cradling him like a newborn baby in his arms. As they entered the room together, Nephrym's heart raced with fear and anticipation.

Nylissa led Auorak into a room that looked to be a massive library. "I think you will find this suitable," she said and smiled at him. Auorak looked around, taking in the vast knowledge collected here. The magic pulled at him as if it had never left his side. He could feel every book calling to him, begging to be read. "Yes, this will do quite nicely," he said, smiling broadly.

As he stepped deeper into the room, a soft hum filled the air—an ancient energy that seemed to pulse through the books and the very shelves. His fingers brushed against the spines of the nearest volumes, and a wave of familiarity washed over him. It's almost as if the books remember me.

And as for Lupine, Barnabiz, Drak, Nephrym and Val? I am so sorry, sweet reader. But this is as much of the story as I am allowed to tell you at this time. Some days, it feels like my pen was dipped in some sort of vile ink and our good virtue as present as an absent father. Today, it was not, and it is way too early in our narrative, and our moral compass is not yet pointing in the direction of such turpitude. If only we would not be branded harlots and deviants. Then, you could read the rest of the story of what transpired behind closed doors.

All you sex-crazed perverts will have to fan fiction it or wait for the unedited version to be told by Barnabiz the Ogre Bard. I know, you're probably thinking, what in the hell could only be told in the unedited version? Use your imagination, and think pervy things. And after you think that your mind has sunk to a level of depravity, you think there could be none worse; think one hundred times worse. Yes, it is actually as mortifying as you're thinking right now. As if you actually had any doubts?

Feeling refreshed with much-needed relief, the party stormed into the general store after the hot bath and other activities. They march through the aisles, gathering every piece of essential equipment and gear that might be needed for the next adventure. Eyes alight with determination and faces ablaze with resolve, each moved rapidly to prepare for what lies ahead.

The shopkeeper, Svenly, strode up to the group, his bright yellow apron smudged with dirt. He cleared his throat and asked what he could do for them. Val'Rak stepped forward and handed Svenly a list of supplies they were in need of. His voice quivered as he added, "We require fresh horses for our expedition. We cannot afford too many days of walking from tired horses if we wish to make our destination on time."

Svenly's bushy eyebrows shot up as he studied Val'Rak curiously from beneath his heavy black eyeglasses. "The stables are on the northern edge of town," Svenly told them as he turned to go back behind the counter. "I will have your supplies ready for you shortly."

"Who needs horses when we can have the mage beside the brothel open a portal to the ruins and give us a scroll to open one back up to Retsnimle's cottage?" Asked Auorak as they were preparing to go to the stables in search of steeds.

Drak's face twisted in exasperation as he let out a heavy sigh. "I am perfectly fine with it," he said through gritted teeth. "Anything to speed up this gods' forsaken journey."

"Aye! I am all in. Besides, Ogres and horses are not a good mix. Hard to find one that is ogre-sized."

So, it looks as if the plans have changed. The party decided it would employ the use of a portal, hopefully. But first they must go back into the back to the general store to pick up their much-needed supplies. And then it looks as if our group of not-so-weary travelers shall finally be on their way.

Svenly's face lit up with a warm smile as the adventurers entered, and he bowed his head in respect. He then started placing bags of supplies on the counter, rattling what sounded like metal pieces. "Welcome back, my dearest patrons! I have everything you requested, plus a few extras Retsnimle asked me to add."

With a sigh, Lupine shoved away from the small general store counter and pushed back his chair. With an exaggerated yawn, he called out that this "crap" was boring and said he was going to the tavern for a quick ale. He didn't even look behind him as he stepped outside into the warm summer air, leaving his companions grumbling in their wake.

The streets of the village were quiet, save for the distant murmur of voices from the tavern and the soft rustling of leaves in the gentle breeze. Lupine inhaled deeply, enjoying the brief solitude. He wasn't much for crowds or idle talk, preferring the company of his thoughts over the constant chatter of his companions. His boots scuffed lightly against the cobblestones as he turned the corner, mind already on that first cold sip of ale.

But his moment of peace didn't last long.

He had barely taken two steps out the door when he collided with a young lad, no more than eleven years of age. The force of the impact knocked them both into a clumsy embrace, arms and legs twisted together in a hopelessly tangled web.

"Hey, watch where you're going, gobbie!" Yelled the young boy. "I do not want your stench on me!"

Lupine

Lupine's face turned a deep shade of crimson, and his fists balled up at his side. "You best watch your foul little tongue," he spat out through gritted teeth, "or I will carve it out of your ugly little blonde head." He slowly rose from the ground, never taking his eyes off the other person, and carefully reached onto his side. His fingers wrapped around a cold handle, and he pulled out a sharp silver dagger.

The young blonde boy stepped closer, his face twisted in an inhuman sneer. His eyes were like two cold stones as he spoke, voice low and menacing. "Are you threatening me? I could kill you right here in the street, and no one would care. Hell, I bet they wouldn't even take the time to remove your dead carcass from the street." He paused for effect, letting his words sink in.

The goblin stepped closer to the kid, hissing through sharp yellow teeth. His eyes narrowed and bulged, breathing out a putrid smell as he warned, "Kid, you're about to piss me off. You ever seen a pissed-off goblin? Not pretty. Not pretty at all."

The tall, lanky boy's face was red with anger, and his eyes were full of rage. He jabbed a finger toward the smaller goblin, who took an instinctive step backward. "Who are you calling kid gobbie? My name's Adolfonz. Remember it so when your friends ask who stomped your sorry gobbie ass, you know what to tell them."

For those who may not know, the term "Gobbie" is the most derogatory thing you can call a goblin. Our group of adventuring friends was about to see some of the dark underbelly of the Land of Dodd. A part where racism and hate were all too common. What Lupine did not realize was that the young lad was right. He could slay Lupine and leave his body in the street, and nobody would care. The only inconvenience for them would be if they had to step over him.

"I tell you what, you homicidal little blonde bastard. If you fuck off right now, I may not kill you in your sleep tonight after I show your mom the time of her life."

Lupine's face contorted as he felt a sharp blow to his chin and tumbled backward. He was shocked to see the large boy looming over him, eyes blazing with anger. The young lad wasted no time in unzipping and raining yellow humiliation down on Lupine beneath him while the crowd of onlookers that had gathered around them recoiled in horror and disgust.

Lupine's eyes bulged with rage as he screamed, spittle-flecked on his lips. "This motherfucker just pissed on me! I am gonna gut him and feed his entrails to his kin!" With a swift movement, Lupin raised his knee up and swiftly planted a foot into the exposed crotch of the young boy.

Jumping to his feet, Lupine raised the dagger above his head in a wild gesture, the blade glinting menacingly in the sunlight. The young lad took a step back and swallowed hard, fear plain to see upon his face. The young boy realized he might have bitten off more than he could swallow.

The keep from the general store reached out with a thick, calloused hand and grabbed Adolfonz by the scruff of his neck, yanking him away from the goblin gentlemen. With a hard shove, he flung the boy aside, his face stern and unyielding. "Enough Adolfonz! Mind your manners and apologize now!"

The sobbing boy stood before his father, head bowed low and shoulders trembling. His knuckles were white as he clutched the fabric of his shirt, and he couldn't stop the tears streaming down his face.

"Papa," he whimpered. "The goblin attacked me. He tried to put his hands on me in a naughty way." The lad sniffled pitifully, hoping desperately that his father would believe him.

The man's face darkened, his jaw tightening as he knelt down to the boy's level. "Where did this happen?" he asked, his voice low but simmering with barely contained rage. His eyes searched his son's face for any sign cf deception, but all he saw were trembling lips and tear-filled eyes.

Lupine felt a chill run through his body as he spoke. He glanced away from the father's piercing gaze and shifted nervously. "Sir, I swear on my life, I never laid a hand on your beautiful, young son." He could feel the sweat gathering on his brow and wished he had chosen his words more carefully.

"Nevertheless, Retsnimle will make it all good." The shopkeep's eyes hardened as he pushed his son into the shop with a stern look and whispered, "Shut up," his voice restrained but thick with anger as he remembered who it was he would be dealing with if this went badly.

Lupine all of a sudden realized that apparently their little gnome benefactor pretty much owned this town. What he did not realize is it was not Retsnimle at all but the people he worked for.

They make their way down the cobblestone path to the small, quaint mage shop. It is not much of a store, just a few shelves and display cases with mostly mundane wares. Much to their surprise, when they walk in, behind the counter is none other than Retsnimle himself.

"Good evening, my fine adventuring friends. I see you have finally made your way here to be teleported to the ancient ruins."

"Gather into a tight formation, and away you will go."

"Dos anyone else have an odd feeling that we are not entirely in the loop and what is going on here?" Drak asked. The party, still in disbelief, stood in a tight huddle and waited for the magic to begin. A

63

strange hum filled the air and began to build to a crescendo. Bright fluorescent-hued light glowed from beneath their feet, growing brighter and brighter until it blinded them with its intensity.

Their stomachs had nearly settled before their sight had returned. Before anyone could move a muscle, the air was thin and almost liquid. When their vision finally clears to the point where they can see one another again, they find themselves in a totally different location. The vegetation has taken on a more tropical look, and the air hangs heavy with humidity. They were indeed in the middle of the ancient elven ruins.

Val'Rak surveyed the terrain with a critical eye. He pointed to a clearing carpeted with soft grass and sheltered by a thicket of tall trees in its middle. "We'll make camp here," he said, voice low and wary. "Gather your belongings, and let's get set up quickly – I don't like the feeling in this place. We need to be prepared for whatever awaits us in these ruins."

"Impressive. It appears you may possess a shred of worth after all," Drak sneers as he roughly unpacks his belongings. His sharp words cut through the air like a blade, challenging Val to prove his value to him.

"And I am starving. I am hungrier than a wolf," Nephrym says as he starts to gather wood to start a campfire.

The party, young Val'Rak included, all burst out in laughter. But alas, little Nephrym had no idea what he said. And the irony was wasted.

"Hungry as a wolf or hungry for a wolf?" Lupine snickered as he started to unpack as well.

Barnabiz's eyes twinkled mischievously as he began setting up camp with the others. "I'm sure Wolfy here will be more than happy to satisfy your hunger," he said, nodding at the wolf. "Are you on an all-meat diet?"

Before Barnabiz can set his pack on the ground, Val'Rak is upon him, swords drawn. He puts the tip of one sword against Barnabiz's throat, not piercing the skin. "My, aren't we a wee bit sensitive?"

"I'm so sick of all these stupid jokes about Nephrym and I! It was funny for a while, but now it's just annoying. What we do is our own business – no one else's. What gives anyone else the right to judge us?!" Val'Rak screamed in frustration.

"Hey, you need to calm down right fucking now if you want to be a part of this group," he snarled. The words spitting from Lupine's lips were like bullets fired at close range. "And just so you know, if you can take a dick, you sure as hell better be able to take a goddamn joke." His eyes narrowed in cold amusement as he waited for a response.

Val'Rak's face contorted in a snarling grimace as he muttered to himself, "It isn't fair. All these people judge me and do not know what I am truly capable of. If they only knew that I could tear them apart in an instant, maybe they would think twice before judging. But why can't I control the anger and hunger? It taunts me like a relentless temptation, daring me to give in and let it overtake me." He glanced up and saw Nephrym watching from a distance, and he narrowed his eyes with a smirk and started to smile. Thank the gods for Nephrym.

65

Without him, he did not know how he would survive. There was something about Nephrym that seemed to make the inner turmoil somewhat manageable.

Nephrym shouts in exasperation as he goes and forcefully grabs Val by the leg, wrenching him away from Barnabiz. He screamed at everyone, "Seriously, you all? Now is NOT the time!" His voice was rising to a fever pitch, growing more frustrated; he continued, "Val! Calm down! You know they are just teasing you! They don't mean anything by it!"

"And besides, if you remember correctly, I was not the one taking a dick! You, big ogre fuck! Get the facts straight. And do not think you're fooling anyone. You're about as straight as a meandering river." Laughed Val'Rak as Barnabiz looked at him in awe. Perhaps the lad will be able to carve out a niche within their group, Barnabiz thought. Or perhaps he would have to crush his skull in as he slept one night. The verdict was yet to be determined.

The party, as they set up their camp, was enveloped by a palpable sense of wonder as they took in their surroundings. The ruins loomed ominously, a testament to the ancient power that once ruled these lands. The ancient tropical forests whispered with an eerie quiet that left them all questioning just what kind of evil lurked within. But it wasn't all fear and apprehension; magic crackled through the air like electricity, so powerful it could almost be tasted on the tongue and felt like a thousand tiny fingers dancing over their skin.

As they set up camp, the party couldn't help but ponder what this place must have looked like many years ago before time and decay had laid waste to its beauty. Their thoughts were interrupted by the sound of rustling coming from the east side of the camp, and in unison, they knew what was about to begin.

Bryan Kurt Dodd

Chapter 5

A Tiger By the Tail/Goblin Gets His Grove Back

The party jumped as Barnabiz shouted, "Look, lively girls! We have company!" He pulled out his massive war maul and stepped to the east side of the camp. The rest of the group blinked and gasped as a figure emerged from the undergrowth.

Lady Selise Brightwood

A young elf woman wearing crimson plate armor stood before them. Her face was smooth, with long auburn hair cascading down her shoulders, and her bright violet eyes were both mysterious and breathtaking. Despite her youthful appearance, she emanated power. She strode confidently into the camp, letting her hands linger on the hilts of her sheathed short swords. Her lips curved into a half-smile as her gaze fell upon Nephrym and his companions.

With one eyebrow raised, she asked, "Well, hello, boys and cow." She closed the distance between them in an almost predatory way and sniffed the air around him. "You left me for a gnome? I thought you had better taste than that. Tsk, tsk, tsk."

Nephrym's heart raced as the elf lady confronted him. Her voice was playful, but her eyes held a dangerous gleam as they flicked from Nephrym to the others. The tension in the camp thickened like a storm about to break. Nephrym shifted his weight, his hand twitching toward his weapon, but he hesitated, unsure whether to fight or flee.

He tried to brush off her words, but he couldn't shake the unsettling feeling she was somehow connected to Val'Rak. It was a burning hatred that he couldn't understand - something about her triggered a visceral reaction within him.

Despite his inner turmoil, he kept up a facade of confidence and composure. But with every hateful glance she cast his way, his resolve faltered, and the anger grew stronger. Was it possible that she held some sort of power over him? The thought made his blood boil. He had to get to the bottom of this, one way or another.

The elven lady leaned close to Nephrym, prodding his nose with a long, delicate finger. Her voice was low and mocking as she said, "Well, aren't we a spunky little thing? I suppose that's why Val likes you so much—you get all riled up when he's pounding his cock in and out of your tight little gnome ass of yours? You're just a thrall to be used for his pleasure and then tossed aside like a dirty rag when he tires of you. Just like the dozens and dozens before you."

She paused, letting the weight of her words sink in, her gaze boring into the gnomes. "But don't worry," she added with a cruel smirk, "Your time will come soon enough—if you survive long enough to see it."

Nephrym opened his mouth to retort, but the elf lady cut him off, her face creased with disgust as she stepped closer. "The smell of you two is unbearable. I can tell what you've been up to—you're like animals! At least have the common decency to bath afterward."

"So that you know, there was a lot of bathing involved. Before, during, after…then again after that!" Nephrym spat in her direction.

She sneered. "You know the packs will not accept this—you were supposed to marry me and join our packs, but instead, you killed more than seventy-five of my kinfolks, and now here you are with a gnome? That just shows how petty and naive you really are. Do you think your father will ever approve of whatever this is?"

Val'Rak's fists were clenched, and he was seething with rage. He whirled around to face the elven lady, and his voice boomed across the room. "You know not what you are speaking of! You were never anything more than a venomous viper in my life. My only mistake was that I trusted you for too long. And do not speak for my father! Who do you think set me on this journey?" His words were punctuated with a defiant stomp of his boot as he strode away from her.

The elven lady's voice was sharp and accusing as she confronted the group. She slowly pivoted to face them, her hips swaying gracefully, drawing attention to her lithe frame. Her violet eyes glittered in the dim light of the evening, taking in each person in turn with a cool, appraising gaze. "Hello, everyone. Allow me to introduce myself since dear Val has failed to do so. I am Selise Brightwood, Lady of Alzamon. And until a few weeks ago, Val's fiancé."

"Maybe we should be trying to get some of that gnome ass," Laughed Barnabiz as he turned towards Val'Rak. "I mean, you left her for the little gnomekabob?"

As he pointed first at Selise, then Nephrym, "You are hiding something in your little gnome keester we need to know about, aren't you?"

Val'Rak's face twisted into a grimace of anger and frustration. His hands balled into fists as he struggled to restrain his fury. "This is not how my kind does things, and she knows it," he growled through clenched teeth, struggling to keep his temper in check.

Selise viciously prods Val'Rak, her words dripping with maliciousness and contempt. "What do you think Daddy will do when he finds out your little toy is not even a were? Thankfully for all of these peasants, the Blood Moon clouds even his judgment." Her tone is taunting, her eyes alight with the thrill of confrontation as she watched Val'Rak's every move, waiting for his reaction. Despite the rage bubbling beneath the surface, Val'Rak held himself back; his patience was pushed to its limits. "But we all know how daddy can get when little Val misbehaves."

Lupine shuffled closer to Selise, peering at her suspiciously. He cleared his throat before speaking.

"Quick question," he began, scratching the back of his neck nervously.

"You're a were-whatever as well, right? So, is 'bitch' a derogatory remark toward you or affectionate, as in, like talking about a little puppy dog?" His face softened into a smirk, revealing not only genuine curiosity but insult as well.

"Don't test me, goblin. I will gut you and feed you your entrails and force feed what's left to the cow."

"Who!!! Calm down, sugar tits. Help a goblin out. I could show you things you never thought possible. You know what I'm saying, baby?" Lupine couldn't help but flirt as he was awestruck by Selise's sheer beauty.

"Hey, baby! Goblin Daddy does not give you what you want. Goblin Daddy gives you what you need. And frankly, you need some of me! All of me!"

"Eww! Nasty little goblin," Selise said as she brushed off Lupine's advance. "As if anything of the sort would ever happen." She held her hand up and looked at Lupine. Selise turned on her heel, stepping behind him. As she walked past him, she bent down low and whispered in his ear. "I would as soon rut with a filthy pig," Selise said as she circled her index fingers around the hilts of her two short swords.

Drak's face twisted with anger at the sight of her gripping the pommels of her swords, revealing glinting fangs in his dragon-like maw. He grasped the handle of his war hammer so hard that his knuckles turned white. "Like you could if you wanted to," he spat, spittle flying from his lips.

"You filthy were bitch!" The air was thick with tension as they stood facing each other, ready for anything. "Draw your swords and see what happens!"

Selise turned her back on the group, her laughter echoing through the dense undergrowth of the forest. As she walked away, her footsteps barely rustled the fallen leaves, a strange power emanating from her like heat waves in the desert.

The group was left standing there, frozen, as if they were rooted to the ground. Suddenly, Selise stopped and looked over her shoulder with a sly smile. "They are all yours! Get'em, boys!" she called out before disappearing into the woods. The party knows better than to try and chase an elf down in the forest.

Especially a lycanthrope elf. By the gods, what had they gotten themselves into? The shadows seemed to move with her, bending the forest to her will as if the very trees conspired in her favor. Every rustle of leaves, every snap of a twig, made their hearts race faster. They weren't hunting her—they were the ones being hunted now.

As she went, the ground began to vibrate from the thunderous sound of four sets of paw steps heading straight for camp. The adventurers looked around wildly as giant shadows appeared from behind trees, and suddenly, four of the largest tigers any of them had ever seen materialized in the clearing.

These were no ordinary cats; their coats shone a deep orange-brown, and the size of their teeth was intimidating.

The Tigers

They growled menacingly, saliva dripping from their impressive jaws, ready to attack. Barnabiz bellowed with delight as he swung his war maul into the ribcage of one of the unsuspecting monsters. The sickening crunch echoed through the air, and the creature let out a shrill cry of agony before it collapsed to the ground.

Nephrym and Lupine both dove into action, attacking another of the beasts in a frenzied attempt to bring it down first. One of the hulking monstrosities leaped from its feet and lunged at Drak, pinning him to the ground. Suddenly, a streak of ebony lightning shot through the air and struck the beast right between the eyes, sending it tumbling off Drak. He didn't miss a beat; as soon as he was free, he grabbed his hammer and brought it crashing down onto his attacker's skull with a thunderous force, killing it instantly.

"You're welcome, lizard licker!" Yelled Auorak as he readied another spell.

Nephrym and Lupine climbed onto the back of one of the remaining beasts, each of them armed with daggers. Lupine grinned as he readied his weapons.

"Hey man, this one is mine. Besides, you don't like pussy, remember?" His chuckle echoed through the air as he thrust both daggers into the shoulder blades of the beast.

Nephrym strutted nonchalantly, puffing out his chest and flexing as he boasted about the number of admirers vying for his attention. With a devious smirk spread across his face, Nephrym unsheathed one of his gleaming daggers and jabbed it into the side of the saber-toothed tiger. The wounded beast groaned in agony before collapsing to the ground, its sudden movements sending both Nephrym and Lupine flying through the air.

The remaining beast let out a terrified roar before bounding off into the darkness of the woods, leaving an eerie stillness in its wake. An eerie silence settled, the kind that numbs your heart and sends a cold shiver crawling across your skin, each second stretching with the weight of unseen dread. The party's camp was heavy with unease as if the air itself was trying to warn them away.

"Leave it to the elves to officially build the creepiest place on all of Dodd," Drak commented as he plopped down on a stump and wiped his brow with the back of his arm.

"Elves have not inhabited this forest for over two thousand years. Therefore, they have had virtually no effect whatsoever upon said creepiness," Stated Auorak as he gathered up some broken branches and twigs to start a fire.

"My goodness, what would we ever do without your witty banter to entertain us?" Barnabiz said as he walked towards the rest of the group. He knelt beside the pile of kindling they had collected and arranged on a small patch of earth, then glanced at Auorak with a smile.

"A quick observation and tip. A campfire is usually more efficient when lit." The words had barely left his lips when a fiery bolt shot from Auorak's fingertip, igniting the pile with a crackle and sending flecks of sparks into the night air.

Auorak perched himself on a log beside the blazing campfire, his laughter rumbling up from his belly and echoing in the night air. He met the anxious gazes of the group with an amused smirk.

"Just so we're all clear," he said, his hands dancing in the firelight as he spoke, "I don't think this is gonna end well. You know, like… some of us might not make it out alive sort of well."

Lupine, rummaging through Auorak's tattered bag, gave him a disgusted look. "Wow! How to try your hand at encouragement there, Spell Chucker. Why not go all the way to the negative side and say we are absolutely fucked? I think from now on, we will call the negative side the 'dark side'; it has a nice ring to it huh? Why do you always have to go all dark side on us, Auorak? Well?"

Barnabiz let out a derisive snort and rolled his eyes. He leaned back and ran a hand over his bald head. "Sounds corny as hell," he said, a smirk playing at the corners of his lips. He narrowed his eyes at the two creatures, a wolf shifter and a gnome.

"Let me guess, there is also a light side where everything and everyone is rainbows and fucking sunshine?" he continued, voice dripping with sarcasm.

"Nope. Totally gay as hell." He paused for a moment before adding, "No offense, wolf boy and gnomekabob."

Barnabiz then moved to rummage through his backpack for something to eat.

"Like you could have come up with something better, you rank ogre bastard," Lupine said, not wanting to pass up a chance to pester the large ogre.

"My father was a great ogre, goblin. Don't forget that. He had the brain of a child and could hardly form words, but he was still an ogre. A fearsome ogre warrior."

When none of the party was bickering, things got too quiet. The kind of quiet makes you think you are being watched regardless of if you are or not. And the party couldn't help but keep playing back with the elf Selise had said while she was in camp. Little did they know, she had done her job. She had sown the seeds of distrust and doubt. And the seeds she had sown were already starting to grow.

Auorak leaned forward, his eyes gleaming in the flickering firelight. "So," he said firmly as he neatly folded a scarf and placed it into his bag. "I think it is time our new friend comes clean and tells us exactly what exactly he is and where he is from. And I mean everything. It is obvious now that there is far more to your tale than you or your father has told us." He locked eyes with Val before settling back into the warmth of the fire.

"I am Lord Vladumir Val'Rak II. Heir to the throne of Gastovy. I turned sixteen cycles of the sun the night of the blood moon. I, like all Gastovians, am a natural-born true lycanthrope.

All true-born Gastovians are. That, however, is where my story takes a dark turn. All members of my ancestral line were cursed by the gods many generations ago. My ancestors were originally all celestial beings and blessed by the Lord of Light himself for generations.

Many generations ago, one of my ancestors, in greed for wealth and power, tried to strengthen our already strong bloodlines. He made a blasphemous pact with a greater demon from the ninth level of the hells. Making us not only celestial but lycanthrope in nature. This angered the Lord of Light. And he, along with the other gods of the Land of Dodd, cursed our bloodline. We are still celestial in nature and, therefore, are virtually immortal. No disease nor cycles of the sun can kill us. We as most werewolves, are blessed with heightened regeneration. We heal nearly instantly. Therefore, we truly almost never die. Cursed to outlive all we love.

The other part of our curse is no one from the house of Val shall ever know the true love of the opposite sex. We cannot reproduce with the opposite sex. Only the males of our line are capable of reproduction, as all offspring are always male. And we can only produce an heir during the blood moon, with a member of the same sex we have a soul bond with. Any other child born from our line will be born weak and ill. Almost always succumbing to an early death. Out of seven brothers, only two survived to make the change."

The party hung upon every word Val'Rak told them, feeling both awe and disgust at the same time. "Both Nephrym and I are children of the Blood Moon. And I am convinced that he is the other half of my soul." What young Val'Rak did not know is that Nephrym possessed one half of the demon Grommellions essence and the other. The demon he fought so hard to control at times was but a shell of what it would become.

Drak shook his head in disbelief, a mixture of fear and excitement rushing through him. "I've only heard of this legend in passing at the monastery. I never thought it was actually true that Gastovians were truly cursed instead of just being odd." He paused briefly before adding, "It's astonishing to think such an old tale could be true."

"Holy fucking hell!" Screamed the ogre.

"For fucks sake, be quiet. And what are you screaming about?" Shushed Auorak as he turned back to Val'Rak.

"The gnome is going to have an ass baby." Laughed the ogre. "He is, isn't he?"

Val'Rak nervously tucked a lock of hair behind his ear as she explained. "Yes, it's true. Nephrym will have a child of the blood moon - a rarity in my family. I'm the only one with this distinction. My lycanthrope brothers are all weaker than I, born under normal moons. Nephrym is still my soul mate, and if either of us were to leave or be killed, we would both perish." He paused for a moment, locking eyes with Nephrym before continuing. "Soul-bonded Gastovians cannot truly be apart - their souls die to join each other in the afterlife."

"But I am not of Gastovia Val. How can this all be true?" Nephrym questioned as he was still trying to grasp the gravity of all that was happening.

"Are we really prepared for what lies ahead?" he murmured, his voice barely above a whisper.

The flickering torchlight cast fleeting shadows on his face, revealing a mix of fear and determination as he searched the faces of his companions for reassurance.

Navine knelt down and wrapped her arms around the little gnome, cradling it in her grip. "And did Nephrym have any say in all of this?" she asked, her voice filled with concern.

Val'Rak shook his head in confusion as he stared at the group. "Yes, he must be a true Gastovian to be soulbond with me," he said but then paused in bewilderment.

"Which is strange in and of itself, seeing as we have no gnomes in Gastovy." His words hung heavy in the air, and for a moment, no one spoke.

"I am... okay. I cannot explain the strange pull I feel towards Val'Rak, but it's like something inside of me has finally made sense. Yet there is also a part of me that doesn't understand why I have this inexplicable connection; part of me wants to turn away and run from this feeling. And just when I feel like I am strong enough to do it. I cannot. Not ever."

Val'Rak dropped to one knee and placed his hands tenderly on the gnome's shoulders. "And the longer we are together, the more intense our bond will get," he said as he leaned in and kissed the gnome gently on the forehead.

"This is some next-level shit here now," Drak remarked under his breath as he sat back down by the fire.

"We should know soon enough if there's a bun baking in the oven," Lupine said as he lightly punched Nephrym on the shoulder, a crooked grin playing on his lips. "Another full moon's coming up—two weeks? Three?" His eyes twinkled with mischief.

The party continued to argue back and forth in hushed tones for hours. For the first time in what felt like years, they could finally kick back and relax. Deep down, each of them, whether they would admit it or not, felt afraid.

Despite their efforts to remain calm, none of them could shake the sensation of being hunted. Their nerves were frayed, and every small sound set their hearts racing. Yet, they pressed on, driven by the same force that had brought them here: curiosity, ambition, and hope that perhaps this discovery would make them legends.

But they couldn't ignore the gnawing thought that in the pursuit of greatness, they might be walking into a trap far more dangerous than they could have ever imagined.

They knew they might have perhaps bitten off more than they could handle. They all knew something or someone lurked about in these massive ruins. And something or someone had immense power.

The power that was either going to be the greatest find of their time, their death, or possibly both.

Chapter 6

Hello Death, Nice to Meet You. Is There Going to be a Baby shower?

The darkness of the night lay still and heavy around the camp, with only a few stars peeking through the canopy of leaves overhead. Despite the peaceful silence, not one of the party members could seem to manage more than a few brief moments of sleep before being woken again by some stray noise or uncomfortable twig under their mattress.

As the bright rays of morning began to make their way through the branches of the ancient tropical forest, Auorak still sat at his post in the center of camp, deep in thought. He couldn't help but wonder why two powerful mages like Reto and Retsnimle had not come here on their own. What was so bad about these old ruins that even they could not simply obliterate them? As much as he wanted to uncover the truth, a part of him wished he had never started this cursed journey.

The cool night air gradually began to warm, and the sky shifted from a deep navy to a bright azure. One by one, our friends stirred and climbed from their sleeping bags, blankets, and pillows. They stretched and yawned as they watched the sun climb higher into the horizon. After this day, nothing would ever be the same.

"Wow, you would think this place would be a little less ominous in the daytime. Not so much." Barnabiz reDraks as he started to stow all his gear away in his knapsack.

Barnabiz

Drak looked around the party with a disbelieving expression. "So, let me see if I've got this right," he began, raising an eyebrow. "Reto is dead; we're working for this mysterious Retsnimle character now, and then, out of nowhere, a werewolf boy just showed up at our cottage. He and that little gnome got completely plastered and then started fooling around, waking us all up in the process!

After that, he decided to come along with us here to these elvish ruins where his ex-lover ambushed us...have I missed anything?" He furrowed his brow and started stowing away his gear. "Because if I'm dreaming all of this stuff...just kill me now."

"You forgot the crazy ass satyr thing thinking he is a dragon," Laughed Lupine as he climbed down from the tree he slept in all night.

Lupine

"Your tiny ass is gonna fall off your perch one of these nights," Laughed Nephrym.

"Quick question. If a goblin falls out of a tree to his death and no one is around to hear or see it, did it happen?" Val'Rak asked as he tried unsuccessfully to be whimsical and break the ice this morning.

"Quick question. If the goblin guts the were fag in his sleep and his entrails become his out trails and he dies a quick and horrible death, yet I am the only one to see it because it was me, did it happen?" Lupine snapped back at Val'Rak.

Val'Rak grunted under his breath, "One of these days, I am going to eat you. You little goblin bastard."

"Oh! I am sorry. Should I have said we were homosexual? You must be monarchally correct these days, Your Highness," Laughed

Lupine as he doubled into a ball on the ground, tears streaming down his face. He was laughing so hard.

The corners of Barnabiz's lips twitched as he spoke, and his eyes glinted mischievously. "Honestly, if I was in your position, I'd be more afraid he's gonna 'bugger me' if I bent over like that."

Lupine jumped up from his seat, his beady eyes fixed on Nephrym. He scurried over like a territorial goblin. His chest puffed out as he tried to loom as intimidatingly as his small stature would allow.

"You need to put a leash on your puppy!" Lupine barked, punctuating each word with a poke of his long, sharp finger into Nephrym's chest.

Drak crossed his arms over his chest and glared at the bickering pair. His voice was a low growl filled with exasperation. "Both of you! Cut it out! We're about to venture into an ancient ruin, and from what I know, that means all sorts of dark and evil shit dwells inside. And, if we've learned anything from our past adventures, our luck tends to be less than stellar. So, let's put aside your quarrel and focus on getting this done."

Val'Rak bowed his head in a show of respect before straightening himself and extending his hand out to Lupine. "Drak is right, Lupine. I was way out of line, and I offer my sincerest apologies for saying that I wanted to eat you." His voice was solemn, his face painted with regret.

Lupine raised an eyebrow, crossing his arms over his chest. "Apology accepted... but let's make it clear that if you try that again, I'll be the one having a Val'Rak stew for dinner." A faint smile played on his lips, though his eyes still held a spark of warning.

Val'Rak chuckled softly, relieved by the lighter tone. "Fair enough. Consider the menu permanently revised."

Lupine's hands were clammy as he reached out to take Val'Rak's, and his laughter was forced. "Ok. I accept," he said nervously. "Remember, though, our appetite is heavy, and we are messy eaters. The ogre said so."

After most of the morning packing up their gear, the party was now ready to start their descent into the ancient elven ruins. When they first arrived at the site, they were amazed that nature had reclaimed most of the buildings.

After all the years of abandonment, it was indeed a dungeon. Trees and roots grew and wrapped around buildings while vines adorned every surface. Things kept getting more and more dilapidated, delving deeper and deeper into the ruins. Time had long since forgotten this god's forsaken place.

The party began their descent down the winding stairwell. The silence was punctured only by the clomping of iron-shod boots and the occasional sharp intake of breath.

Everyone was on edge – excited but apprehensive. It had been several years since they had ventured into a dungeon, and no one was sure if they still had what it took to get out alive. The oppressive darkness closed in around them, and each step further inward felt like a march into an unknowable abyss.

"It just keeps getting stranger and creepier as we go further down,"

Nephrym muttered to himself as the group proceeded down the stairs. There was an eerie feeling in the air, and it was like the deeper they went, the more nightmarish it became.

Drak's face was illuminated by the dancing torch in his hand, its light flickering off his grim features. He let out a sigh and shook his head before continuing. "We've already seen what this world has to offer - werewolves, weretigers, all kinds of creatures that we never thought possible. So now it feels like whatever is left is going to be run-of-the-mill stuff for us, you know? Nothing to really grab our attention or shock us anymore."

"Thanks, you lizard-lipped shit for brains. Now you have done it. You have gone and cursed us. Who knows what weird ass stuff we are going to get eaten by now?" Barnabiz shook his head.

The air was thick with a magical aura. The ruins hummed with power, seeping from the walls like a slow-moving mist and swirling around the members of the party. An unnatural stillness cloaked the space, amplifying the slightest sound and making it boom through the eerie silence. Even the bravest of our adventurers could not shake off a sense of unease.

"Are we trekking into the bowels of hell?" Barnabiz grumbled, his head almost hitting the low ceiling as he had to duck in certain spots.

"And put out those fucking torches. Why not send a signal up ahead and tell whatever is down here we're coming? And besides, it's already hot as balls down here." It seemed the heat from the torches' light made the air even thicker.

"I knew the ogre was a poofter. Always talking about wangs and bollocks," Chuckled Lupine as he gingerly walked his way to the front of the party.

The rest of the group stifled their laughter, but a few snickers escaped. Drak shook his head, smirking as he adjusted his grip on his axe. "Careful, Lupine or the ogre might take that as a challenge."

Lupine flashed a grin over his shoulder. "Please, I'd outrun him before he could even think about it."

Val'Rak rolled his eyes, muttering under his breath, "You all better hope he doesn't hear you."

The party stumbled down the treacherous stairs for what felt like an eternity until they reached a door carved with intricate dragon designs. When they opened the door, their gasp was nearly simultaneous as they entered a vast chamber, its walls covered in even more detailed and captivating carvings of dragons. The source of the faint blue light soon came into view – a fountain in the center of the room filled with glowing, ethereal water.

The Fountain

"Glowing blue water…Well, shit got a little bit weirder. Hey Nephrym, I will pay ya a gold piece if ya skinny dip in the fountain." Said Barnabiz as he was flipping a gold coin up in the air repeatedly.

"See, and all of you are worried about a kid. I am telling you. The ogre is into some strange shit. And by strange shit, I think he is jealous little Val railed the gnome before he did." ReDraks Lupine as he pulled out a gold coin and started flipping it in the air as well. "Anyway, I will make it two gold coins, Nephrym."

"What, you guys think I am some cheap whore here to amuse you guys on a whim." Nephrym turned his back on the dastardly duo of would-be voyeurs "Make it five gold pieces, and you got yourself a deal."

Val'Rak threw ten gold pieces into the fountain. "How about ten, but you have to fish them out?" Val really just wanted another peek at Nephrym nude.

Drak's hand waved emphatically in the air as his face twisted into a mixture of annoyance and disbelief. "Holy fucking hell," he muttered under his breath before raising his voice to address the group. "We are never going to get anything done at this rate. I mean, come on now. Val's a teenager, so that comes with the territory. But the rest of you should really be able to act more mature than this - at least half your age."

The ogre smiled, his tusks on full display as he shook with laughter. "I figured you'd be excited to see a gnome skinny dipping in your pond! After all, you are a priest and all. He looks like no more than a child!" His low, guttural laugh echoed through the dense dungeon air.

Drak admonished the ogre with a pointed finger, reminding him that he was indeed a priest—a dragon-born priest. "Don't forget that we feast on children of our enemies, not force ourselves upon them," he corrected.

The only sound that echoed in the grandiose and eerie chamber lit by a blue, glowing fountain was that of the splashing water as a petite, naked gnome darted around frenetically collecting the gold coins cast by Val'Rak. His wiry frame shone in the dim light as he dived and twisted, eddying around the fountain.

Nephrym surfaced, pushing his wet hair away from his face, and wiped his mouth with the back of his hand. "Other than tasting a little funny, this water is not bad," he said, taking a moment to savor the pleasant sensation of it on his skin before diving again in search of gold coins.

Val'Rak slowly stepped towards the fountain, his heavy boots thudding with each step. He reached out a hand as if to caress the water's surface. His fingers tightened, and he scooped the tiny gnome out of the fountain like a lost toy. He cradled him like an infant in his great arms and dug into his bag of supplies for a cloth rag.

Val'Rak could smell the healing water before they entered the room. It was a scent he was familiar with, having spent many days in the royal herbalist's potion-making laboratory down the hallway from his quarters. His gnome companion clung to him, and as Val'Rak placed the tiny figure onto the ground, he warned him.

"You should get dressed. Everyone is already jealous. And I do not like to share." He carefully dried off his wet limbs and body before setting him down cn the edge of the fountain.

Nephrym's eyes widened as he felt an unfamiliar warmth wash over him. He had never in all his ninety-six years of life felt this way towards a member of the same sex before. His vision blurred, his cheeks flushed, and he felt a powerful desire to be near Val'Rak, but he couldn't help but wonder - was it just his own emotions or was some sort of magic at play? All he could do was look into Val'Rak's enchanting blue eyes and try to make sense of the bewildering feelings that threatened to overtake him.

"That's it, little man. Get dressed so your pup can roll his tongue back in and start scouting again," Drak said with a chuckle as he inched closer to the fountain. His eyes widened when he heard that this fountain had healing liquid inside. "Did I hear that right? These fountain's waters are healing quaff."

Val'Rak reached into his rucksack, carefully selecting a large flagon and then filled it with the striking blue liquid. "Yes," he said, as he looked around at the others, "This was a concoction I had to smell daily in my childhood. That is why I have no objections to Nephrym joining us here. The castle apothecary and some of the clerics were fond of this elixir."

Auorak observed Val'Rak from across the room. The young man had a look of mystery about him, something he couldn't quite put into words. He watched as Val'Rak fidgeted with a piece of string, his eyes darting between Auorak and the floor as if he was trying to hide something. "There is more to you, young Val'Rak, than you let people

95

know," he said. The party was unaware of the complex origins of their companion, Val'Rak. His bloodline had been cursed and blessed by the gods of Dodd, causing a mix of celestial and demonic power to course through his veins. Val'Rak had given them the abridged version, but even that small amount raised the alarm in the sorcelock's awareness.

Val'Rak looked solemnly at Auorak, his eyes filled with both mystery and gravity. "The true nature of House Val's lineage and history is never shared with anyone," he said in a muffled voice. "Upon becoming king, all knowledge of House Val is bestowed upon the new king the instant the crown is placed upon his head." He paused for a moment, scrutinizing Auorak's face before continuing. "I told you all I know."

Auorak

Lupine stood before Val'Rak with a mischievous glint in his eye. His small goblin hands were clasped tightly together, and he leaned forward eagerly as he asked, "What if someone were to acquire your crown? Would they know all of House Val's dirty little secrets when it was placed upon their head?"

Val'Rak stood before Lupine, his eyes heavy with warning. "No, the previous king must be dead. And the new king must be of true Val lineage. Otherwise, when the crown is put upon your head, it will take your life as no mortal can possess the profound authority and power it embodies." His hand slowly lifted toward Lupine's temple and gave him a gentle pat as he then turned away from him.

A dry, soft chuckle escaped Val'Rak's lips as he removed one of his many rings and tossed it across the room in Lupine's direction. "Besides," he said, shaking his head with amusement, "it would never fit on your tiny head. Here, this should fit you better than my father's crown."

Barnabiz sauntered over to Val'Rak. His face twisted into a smirk. He bent down on one knee and looked up at the prince with inquisitive eyes. "So, are you the oldest? First in line for the throne?" His voice was light and mocking. "Or are you some spoiled little puppy prince out to sow his royal oats before getting married off to some wench your dad picks for you? We've all been through that phase," he added, chuckling.

Val'Rak's eyes flashed in anger as he squared his shoulders and faced the giant ogre. His clenched fists trembled at his sides as he shouted, "Phases? What are you speaking of, ogre? I assure you that

Nephrym is not some phase I am going through! You best watch your tongue lest I cut it out of that gaping, tusked asshole you call a mouth." He gestured wildly with his hands, emphasizing each word. "And I told you everything I know about my family line. And no, I am not the oldest, but I am the heir to the throne of Val!"

Navine's face was a deep shade of red, and her hands were clenched into fists. She let out an exasperated sigh before walking determinedly towards the door opposite the fountain.

"Enough already!" she yelled over her shoulder, "We have to keep moving if we ever want to complete this quest. Learning about young Val'Rak can wait. We have more pressing matters to attend to right now."

Navine had not even taken two steps through the arched doorway when she heard a loud whooshing sound and felt a searing heat. She looked up to see a blazing fireball hurtling toward her. In an instant, it collided with her chest plate and sent her flying back into the center of the room. She crashed into the deep blue fountain with a loud splash.

Lupine leaped up with a fist pump as the minotaur paladin flew into the air and splashed down in the fountain, sending a geyser of droplets cascading around them. "Score!" he yelled.

"That's it. Let everyone in this god's forsaken place know we are here, you little red bastard," Muttered Auorak under his breath, trying to be quiet.

"Hello, flaming ball to the chest. I think the ship has sailed, genius. You ignorant little goblin shit. It was a trap. But we would have known if the thieves were actually doing their damn job." Drak yelled out.

"Ohhhhhhh. I did not think of that." Lupine crossed his muscular arms and cocked his head, a look of confusion spread across his tanned face. His eyes searched the room as he realized Drak's words had been an insult to his intelligence and ability as a thief. He settled on a weak smile as he shrugged.

Lupine clenched his fists and bared his jagged teeth, taking a menacing step toward Drak. His face was a deep crimson as he spat his words. "How dare you question my rogue prowess! I may be an ignorant little goblin shit, but I can assure you that I am the best-damned thief in the entire Land of Dodd!" All the while, Drak stood silent, head slightly cocked to the side, a smirk playing upon his lips.

Barnabiz's weathered face was a mask of fury as he unslung the maul from his back and stormed towards the doorway. "For fucks sake!" he roared, "Stop arguing, you two; can't you cast some sort of spell to check for traps magically? Or did you miss that one in mage preschool?" Taking a deep breath, Barnabiz readied himself for whatever dangers lay beyond that threshold.

A loud clank resonated through the chamber as Nephrym and Val'Rak went to aid Navine as she struggled to get free of the fountain. She was dripping wet and slumped in the fountain, her once-shining breastplate charred black at the edges from the flaming sphere.

As they pulled her out of the water, she gasped for air, and light slowly returned to her eyes. Miraculously, the healing properties of the ancient liquid had rapidly repaired even her worst injuries.

Nephrym glanced anxiously at Navine and Val'Rak. His voice shook as he asked, "If there is a fountain full of healing liquid so close to the entrance of this dungeon, what other kinds of horrors lurk beyond?"

Val'Rak let out a heavy sigh, his massive shoulders drooping in resignation. He turned away from Nephrym and stared into the unknown void before them. "No one knows what awaits within its depths. All who enter are never heard from again...That's why I had to come with you, Nephrym—so I could protect you or die with you."

There is so much Val'Rak wished he could tell Nephrym. But, for fear, he would not understand. He simply could not tell him or anyone else the true reason they were in this god's forsaken place. Or that Reto and Retsnimle both worked for his father.

As the party continued its way deeper into the ancient ruins, the cloud of despair grew heavier. Something about this place was off, almost as if it sucked the life and positivity out of you. Everyone noticed, yet no one would acknowledge what was happening.

Dark magic had so permeated everything in this wretched place, and you could almost feel it in the air. But something in here was familiar to our young Val'Rak. He was drawn to this place like a moth to a flame. What he could not tell the others was he had seen this place in his dreams.

Dreams, which were more like visions it was turning out. So far nearly every vision had come to him in his dreams had come to fruition. The rest of the visions had not so far, and those were the ones he was worried about. Was he truly capable of some of the horrific acts he lived out in his dreams every time his eyes closed?

Auorak's luminous eyes shone with a strange light as he made his way through the corridor, his hands tracing along the walls as if searching for something. His lips moved in hushed mutters about harnessing the power of the place, and as he spoke, tendrils of dark smoke curled around his fingers. He was mesmerized by the foul magic that clung to every surface, its potency palpable to him on a level rivaling even gods. "If one could find a way to harness all the magic in this place. The amount of power one would have would be unimaginable."

Drak's face lit up, his blue eyes gleaming. He gestured towards the ruins that encircled them and began to explain in an excited voice. "I think I've read about this place.

According to legend, it was once an elven stronghold, a veritable city of beautiful spires and towers, but the gods destroyed it - they had no choice. You see, the elves were in league with demons and other foul creatures and even conspired against the Lord of Light himself. But the other gods stepped in and saved the Lord of Light at great cost – wiping it all out, an entire civilization never to be heard or seen again. Could this be that very same place?"

The corridor plunged into darkness. Everyone held their breath, and the air grew thick with anticipation. Then, as if pulled from thin air, flame erupted from each of the sconces along the walls, restoring light to the hallway.

Lupine ran his fingers through dark, wirey hair, nervously rocking back and forth on the balls of his feet. He averted eye contact as he mumbled a question about supposed herb usage that morning and if it correlated to the flickering torches lining the corridor wall. His cheeks flushed red as he glanced up at one of the now fully re-lit torches."Ok, I may or may not have smoked two small baggies of halfling herb this morning while everyone was sleeping. If I did, and I am not saying I did. Did, or did not all these damn torches go completely out and light themselves back?"

Nephrym bellowed, eyes wide and face contorting with rage. "You thieving, little goblin bastard! You stole my herb!" He gestured wildly at Lupine, who held his knapsack in hand and had an expression of innocence plastered on his face. Nephrym knew he was referring to the rare halfling herb he had so carefully collected and stored away - which was apparently now gone.

"I was doing you a favor. Your sir, have a drug problem. Look at yourself, man. You are getting drunk and having wild orgies. And the gods only know what other drugs are involved. I mean, you are getting ram-rodded by a sixteen-year-old boy, and let's not forget the whole getting poled by the wolf thing. I mean, you got some issues my friend. And I, being the kindhearted goblin I am, want to help you. And if it means I must smoke bag after bag of halfling weed to keep you from it, so be it." Remarks Lupine from his soapbox as he tries ever so cunningly to cover up the fact he stole Nephrym's halfling weed and smoked it.

"Wow, when you think the level of fucktardivity cannot get any higher. Guess what? It gets higher, literally. And you have the audacity to argue with the werewolf cock sock about stealing his halfling weed. Bravo, Bravo. The award for the most fucktarded goblin goes to...." Barnabiz flamboyantly expressed as he was interrupted by the magical bolt hitting him squarely in the chest.

"Well fucking bollocks. That is going to leave a mark." Barnabiz swung around his massive maul and charged towards the caster, now standing in the corner of the room. In the midst of arguing, no one noticed they were no longer in the corridor but in a large, roughly thirty-foot by thirty-foot room with a tall ceiling. Screams and shouts pierced the air as this fact became evident to all in the room. At once eight black-robed figures were visible amongst the pillars,

wrists raised, palms directed towards each party member in turn.

Val'Rak stepped forward, drawing one of his swords and offering it to Nephrym. As soon as the younger man touched the pommel, it shrank down to fit his size, allowing him to wield it effortlessly. Meanwhile, Val'Rak began to transform. His body rippled with dark energy before morphing into the form of a huge black dire wolf.

DarkWizard

Val'Rak offered Nephrym a broad smile from his fanged muzzle as the gnome struggled to climb onto his back before setting off at a quick trot. A laugh escaped as he said with a grin, "Now let's show them what a gnome on a wolf can do!"

Val'Rak, now a large, four-legged beast with thick black fur and glowing red eyes, lumbered forward as Nephrym brandished his magical sword. Gritting his teeth, Nephrym shouted, "Onward, my furry concubine!" Val'Rak leaped forward, claws bared and snarling, towards one of the enemy magic users.

Auorak's eyes widened, and his brow furrowed as he raised his hands and bellowed an arcane incantation, the words spilling from his lips like fire. A bolt of black energy shot from his fingers and slammed directly into the face of one of the robed casters, erupting into a blaze of purple and black fire.

"Gnome fucker, please," Auorak said, shaking his head and chuckling as he looked around at the other stunned onlookers. "Watch and learn."

Auorak's face broke out in a wide grin as the blaze of purple and black fire engulfed the magic user. He raised his arms triumphantly, already imagining how he'd tell the story later to his friends. Around him, the other combatants paused in awe at the sheer power of his spell. "Killshot!" he shouted confidently.

Val'Rak and Nephrym stopped sharply and turned directly in front of one of them. Nephrym lashed out with the vicious scimitar and struck the magic user in the side. The magic user, who looked to be human, let out an anguished cry of pain as it fell to the ground, clutching its side where the blade landed.

Unfortunately, gravity had other plans for our young gnome rogue. With the sudden turn by Val'Rak and the force of swinging the unfamiliar blade, Nephrym lost his grip on Val'Rak's back and ended up underneath the dire wolf with nothing but a face full of wolf beans and franks if know what I am saying. Nephrym was holding on for dear life, mainly because he had no idea where the damn sword was pointed exactly, and he knew it had the ability to instantly kill but, at the same time, wanted to let go because he knew he would never hear the end of this from his friends.

"Fucking hell, this is what I am talking about. Celebratory fellatio. I am next!" Roared Barnabiz as he skipped towards the next magic user.

"This shit is getting a bit too weird now. I am officially creeped the hell out!" Yelled Drak as he branched off from behind Barnabiz in hopes of surprising one of the robed casters.

Auorak's eyes darted around the room in search of the mysterious robed figures, but they were gone as suddenly as they had appeared. He couldn't help but shiver at the sudden feeling of emptiness and paranoia that filled the air in their wake. He stepped forward cautiously, checking for any hidden magic or clues as to where they might have disappeared.

"Shit! We are in a totally different room again." Barnabiz noticed as he wandered around in the corner, realizing the statue was not there moments ago.

"Everybody stop! Stay where you are!" Yelled Auorak. "All of the rooms have teleportation traps. So far, we have all been teleported together. We do not want to get separated in this gods' forsaken shithole."

"The mage is right," Drak said, gesturing for Nephrym and Lupine to move forward. His words were reassuring yet firm as he continued his instructions. "Everyone stand perfectly still. Nephrym and Lupine can disable all the traps so we can go on safely." The two thieves nodded, their eyes scanning the treacherous room ahead of them.

Lupine let out a wry laugh as he cautiously surveyed the room, his eyes tracing the shadows and crevices of the walls.

"Sorry to burst your bubble, but we ain't that type of thief." He ran his hands along the edges of the furniture, searching for any telltale signs that would reveal how the traps were set up.

"There is so much magic in this damn place. I cannot focus on any one particular thing for long," Muttered Auorak as he strained his abilities in hopes of finding a way to shut off the teleportation.

"I think it is the bloody fucking floor tiles," Barnabiz replied as he stepped on one, and it turned yellow briefly as the party was yet again blinked to another section of the ruins.

"Gods be damned, your fucking stupid." Whispered Val'Rak under his breath.

"What did you say, Vlad Von Gnomefocker?" asked Barnabiz as he stormed toward Val'Rak.

"No, you idiot!" Screamed Auorak and Drak as they were all teleported yet again.

"Oops, was that me?" Barnabiz shrugged, and he stood awkwardly on one foot so as not to touch another floor tile.

The party found themselves in a twelve-foot by twelve-foot room. Torches mounted on each wall cast a blue flame, creating an eerie glow that sent a chill down the adventurers' spines. Noticing three large, ornate chests against one of the walls brought back memories of past misadventures involving mimics and left everyone feeling uneasy.

"Fuck me," Lupine said in his most manly tone. He flopped down in the far corner of the room opposite the chests, and a flurry of kicking arms and legs followed. "I am not going anywhere near those damn things. I swear, mimics have a taste for goblin flesh! They are racist. I saw one eat half a tribe once. Goblin is a mimic delicacy, and I am too young to die!"

"Not every damn chest is a mimic, Lupine," Stated Drak as he softly patted the little goblin on the shoulder to comfort him. "Now pick one and go inspect it for booby traps and let us see what is inside. Hopefully, it will be whatever this Retsnimle guy is wanting so we can get the fuck out of here. And nothing has a taste for goblin flesh; you know that right."

"Nope. Way too easy." Auorak replied as he went over to the middle chest and threw open the lid. Six large, heavily armored knights appeared on the wall adjacent to the chest, with six tower shields and great swords clenched in each hand. They can be heard grunting and grinding their teeth from under their metal masks. "Told you so," Auorak said with a smirk.

"Relax, they are illusions. Look, I can run my hand through this one." Nephrym stated as he was running his arm upward like he was shoving it up into the armored knight's ass.

"Again, with the ass play." Barnibiz mocked the gnome and winked. "You have a problem, you little butt pirate, purple porthole pickle pirate, rump ranger, I can keep going."

The giant knights of light faded away as quickly as they had appeared and were gone with the sudden clack of Auorak slamming shut the lid of the large chest. He ran his hands along its exterior, taking in every detail, from the difference in texture between the wooden body and metal hinges to the intricate runes etched into the sides. His well-practiced eyes sought knowledge that might aid them on their journey into the depths. Before this excursion, Auorak felt confident in his ability to decipher ancient secrets.

Lupine's eyes darted around the room, his chest heaving with heavy breaths. He mumbled to himself as he paced back and forth behind Auorak, his finger jabbing accusingly at the air. "Holy cow, am I the only one feeling like we are being pranked? It is that creepy-eyed spell-chucker, I know it. My goblin sense is tingling!"

Drak leaned over the chest to his left, squinting at something and shaking his head. Chuckling, he said, "Goblin sense? Seriously? It's not working out too well for you, huh?" Drak couldn't help but smile as a warmth spread through him.

"I will have you know it has saved my life on many occasions," Boasted Lupine as he reached out and opened the lid on the third chest, which was on the right of the one Auorak had been eyeing for what was like an eternity in goblin time.

The sound of metal grinding against metal echoed through the room as the chest was pried open. A bright blue light filled every corner of the room, causing everyone to shield their eyes in pain as soon as it creaked open. When the light faded, and they opened their eyes again, everything had changed. They were now standing in a circular room with a domed ceiling.

On the ground, in the center of the room, was an intricately carved throne. The detailed carvings depicted werewolves in battle and scenes of wolves howling at an illuminated moon.

Val'Rak's eyes shoot open in terror as he recognizes the strange place. He grabbed Nephrym's arm and urgently cried out, "We can't stay here! We have to go now! Now! We should not be here!" Without another word, Val'Rak yanked Nephrym up and drew him close to him.

Auorak's eyes widened in surprise as he took in the sight of Val'RaK. He surveyed the intricate stone carvings, the massive pillars, and the steep stairs leading to a heavy wooden door. "What is this place?" he asked, turning his gaze back to Val'RaK. "How is it you know about a room in an ancient, abandoned ruin exactly? How have you been here before?"

"We have to go, and I can't explain why! I know you don't understand the danger we are in, but trust me when I say that it's real. We don't have much time left before it's too late, so please hurry!"

Lupine's face had turned a deep crimson, and his breathing came in sharp gasps as if he had just run a marathon. "He's brought us here to turn us into werewolf sex slaves! We are all dead!" he screamed, his voice echoing off the damp stone walls of the underground chamber.

Barnabiz's knuckles turned white, the tendons in his arm bunched up as he swung it back. His hand connected with Lupine's face, and the sound of skin smacking against skin echoed throughout the room. Lupine stumbled backward, then fell to the ground with a dull thud. Barnabiz towered over him, chest heaving, and spat out the words, "Shut your trap, you little goblin twat! Get up and hold yourself together."

Drak's hand slowly slid down to the pommel of his Warhammer as he narrowed his eyes at Val'Rak. His voice was low and menacing as he demanded, "Explain to us how you know what this place is."

Val'Rak trembled as he stood before the throne of the Lich Lord Nivlac. His father's past dealings with this wicked creature echoed like thunder in his mind. He was suddenly aware of the horrific things and terror that lies within these chambers - a darkness so powerful and venomous that it has no bounds.

Val'Rak was overcome by a primal fear, one that could never be quelled and one that would haunt him forever. A fear rooted in knowing that the only way to conquer this type of evil was to pit it against something even more sinister.

"I have been in this very room. Standing in this very place with my father. The only thing missing is the lich that is always sitting on that throne," Val'Rak almost whispered as fear filled his senses as he pointed an unsteady finger toward the empty throne.

"Well, if he is a friend of your dad, maybe he will help us get out of this place."

"You do not understand Nephrym; we have been sent here to steal from him. He will know this. And besides, the last time I was here with my father, he tried to kill all of us."

Barnabiz broke his silence, eyes ablaze. He pointed his maul at the group and bellowed, "You know you could have led with that little gem of info, wolf boy! Prepare yourselves. It looks like we are going to have a mess on our hands before this story sees an end."

"Wait, how exactly did your father and his entourage get here?" Auorak asked.

"Our mage opened a portal, and we all stepped through. This is the only room we ever saw. I had no idea where it actually was. I was just a child. But the lich tried to use dark magic to take my birthright from me."

"For fucks sake. This is exactly what we need in our lives. More fricking magic users!" Yelled Lupine.

Navine gritted her teeth, tugging at the goblin's ear. "Will you shut up?" she hissed through clenched jaws. "If we have any hope of surviving this, you need to shut up. Your constant shouting is going to be the end of us!" The goblin winced, whimpering as Navine released her grip.

"Wait, you said lich?" Drak said. "Why are there scenes depicting werewolves on the walls? It's not some sort of weird-ass were lich or something, is it?" Drak asked as he could not stop staring at the sheer mastery of the carvings.

"No, he is not a lycanthrope. I must tell you all something. Nivlac, the Lich Lord, is not a werewolf. He was an ancient mage with dementia who drove himself to the brink of insanity and used powerful spells to turn himself into a lich. He wielded an enchanted staff with which he could control any lycanthrope in the Land of Dodd, dominating their minds until they were mere puppets dancing for his pleasure. I've seen him force them to battle each other until nothing but piles of corpses remain."

Val struggled to contain his tears as fear clenched like a vice around his heart. He knew his new love and friends would face a fate worse than death if they dared to challenge the mad tyrant. He knew the only way out, and it terrified him. He feared letting the demon in fully. He feared he would lose himself to the demon one day.

Barnabiz slumped his shoulders forward and shook his head. His voice was low and heavy with sadness, in stark contrast to its usual blustering and booming presence. "Pops wanted you dead. Was he so angry at you that he sent you away like a lamb to the slaughter? Not even an ogre father would wish such a fate upon their offspring."

"He cannot control me."

"Well, you're a were a dog, are you not?" Asked Lupine as he and the party members were curious to hear this explanation.

"Well…" "Spit it out, lad. We ain't got all fucking day. There is a mad werewolf-controlling lich coming to kill us all soon!" Expressed Barnabiz, as his patience has worn thin over the last few days.

"I am something different," she said. "Nivlac called me a half-breed and a hybrid, but I'm not sure what that really means. One thing I do know is that he can't control me or my father like he does the other werewolves. Last time he tried, I drained all the power from his staff, temporarily at least."

Drak's gaze drilled into young Val with the intensity of a thousand suns. His voice sharp and demanding, Drak barked, "How many times has he tried?" His words hung heavy in the air, crushing any peace that was present before. "Your father kept bringing you here? What, for the lich to do magical experiments on?"

Barnabiz's boots clacked against the stone floor as he strode over to the young man. "Well, come on then, out with it, lad," he bellowed. "We may be marching to our deaths soon enough, may as well know with whom we march to the executioner." As he spoke, flecks of spittle flew from his lips and peppered the youth's face.

"A few, like five or six." the boy replied, his voice weak and shaky with fear. Barnabiz towered over him, his leathery face twisted into a frown.

Val was trembling with fear. He had just begun to gain acceptance from the group, and now he feared that everything would be taken away from him. What if they all hated him? Or worse, wanted to harm him? Tears began to roll down his cheeks as he imagined Nephrym's reaction when he revealed his true identity. How could he explain it in a way that would make sense to everyone else when it seemed like such an impossible task for him to process himself? Barnabiz stepped forward and plopped down beside Val, exhaling deeply.

Barnabiz felt a twinge of guilt as he barked out his demand, but he knew that if Val could just let it all out in the open, he would be much better off. Still, the coldness of his words hung heavy in the air, and Barnabiz couldn't shake the feeling of being too hard on the young man. "Your old man is a right piece of shit, is he not?"

"How? How can one possibly be more than a werewolf?" Drak whispered in terror, his skin crawling as he considered the possibilities. Never before had he encountered such an idea in all his dark and forbidding studies. Surely, this must herald something sinister and unknown. The dark force behind the scenes was finally starting to rear its ugly head.

"I am part celestial, part demon and a true-born lycanthrope. True born meaning, I can never be cured. My family is cursed by the gods of the Land of Dodd. The gods sought to annihilate our bloodline altogether totally. Decreeing, no heir shall ever be birthed from the House of Val. So, in anger and frustration, my ancestor called out in anguish to any divine being, be they good or benevolent, to help him. To ensure his bloodline would not end with him.

A demon lord by the name of Grommellion answered his call. But as we all know, no deal with a demon comes without dire consequences. From that day forward, the only way for the House of Val to continue its bloodline was in an unnatural and unholy manner.

The demon gave him what he longed for. He bestowed upon my family the gift of being near immortal, powerful, being always attractive and desired by the opposite sex. But at the same time cursed my family line not to be capable of ever loving anyone of the opposite sex.

The only way for us to procreate was with another of the same sex. And then only through Vilemagic and the demon. All dependent upon the blood moon. Planting our seed in them, so to speak. Where it will grow and grow until finally, it will consume the host and eat its way out of its so called shell. The first was my great, great, great grandfather. A child born any other way to the house of Val is cursed never to survive a full cycle of the sun.

The demon took him, and 6 months later, a child was born. And now, we are all those things. Angelic, if you will, demonic and lycanthrope all at the same time. Our bloodline is of both the heavens and the hells and everything in between."

"Well, does explain a few things." Lupine blurted in.

"What a damn minute!" Barnabiz interrupted. "So, you're telling me you knocked up the gnome while you were on a drunken possessed bender?"

"Yes, you dolt. We were given that little tidbit of information a day or so back." Drak explained.

Nephrym stared into Val's eyes, searching desperately for a sign of him understanding how he felt. His heart was pounding, and his body felt jittery - he could feel the truth inside him, calling out to him relentlessly. At first, he thought it was merely dreams, but now he was certain. As if the unborn child, or whatever it was, was speaking to him.

"You are right. We have been so lucky to find one another, even

115

amid all this chaos. I never wanted to hurt you or your friends." Val took Nephrym's hand and squeezed it gently. "You will be part of something historic now. We may be about to change the world." He only hoped it was for the better.

"Okay, okay!" Lupine shot back. "Let me get this straight. The gnome and the wolf went for a stroll on the chocolate pathway, and in about five months or so, there really will be a little demon wolf baby who will eat its way out of Nephrym?" Lupine asked as he was beside himself with laughter and an ever-so-small amount of concern for his friend.

"Yes, but not exactly," Val said as he sat down in front of Nephrym. "I didn't want to have to tell you and worry you so soon. But the baby is going to kill you when it arrives if you don't become a lycanthrope. Given all that's happened, you must undergo the rite of the pack immediately. I can't explain everything right now; just trust me on this. It is the only way for you to gain control and live."

The news was met with a mixture of emotions: joy for their friend who had found love, it seemed and was expecting a child, fear that Nephrym may die if he wasn't transformed into a werewolf, and confusion about what the right course of action might be.

Navine felt overwhelmed, her conflicting emotions threatening to consume her. She wanted to celebrate for her friend, yet the thought of him giving birth to a demonic entity made her feel nauseous. She bent down and hugged Nephrym tightly, sending up a silent prayer for his safety.

Drak's eyes blazed with righteous anger as he towered over Val.

His fists were clenched, and his voice shook with emotion. "You know we cannot let you do this to our friend? You're sentencing him to a life of demonic servitude and damnation. How can you do this if you genuinely love Nephrym? This is the exact opposite of love—this is not what real love looks like."

"It's simple. Val was blindly in love with Nephrym. And Nephrym was blindly in love with Val. Good and evil were battling it out, and they were caught in the crossfire. And as far as Val went, this was all he had ever known. So naturally, he saw nothing wrong with any of this." Auorak tried to explain to Drak.

The party, now terribly distracted, did not notice the four hooded figures step out of the shadows in the corners of the room. All were robed in different colors. The blue-robed mage removed his hood, revealing blond hair and a youthful face with elven ears poking through it.

The four-robed figures stepped forward, and the remaining three removed their hoods and gestured with their hands to the group. "Give the boy and the gnome over to us." The figures' voices blended together in a chilling unison, each syllable echoing through the cave. "The rest may go freely so long as you depart this place."

"Are you fucking kidding me?" Barnabiz roared as he swung his maul from his back. "I was getting into this story, and now you four fuck nuts gotta come and interrupt us. I am gonna teach you assholes some manners. Ogre style!" His eyes narrowed, and a heavy snort bellowed from his chest. He gripped the handle of his weapon with both hands, dug his feet into the ground, and leaned forward, waiting for someone to make a move. His nostrils flared, breathing in deeply through them.

Before Barnabiz could take a step, a blazing fireball flew out of the red-robed figure's hands toward him. It screamed and crackled in the air with unbelievable speed before exploding when it reached its destination and struck his chest. Drak looked on in horror as thick roots and sharp vines erupted from the ground to form an impenetrable wall around him and locked him into place.

Navine and Lupine were blindsided by a towering wall of water suddenly manifesting itself from thin air as the blue-robed figure chanted ancient words. Lastly, Auorak was left alone, standing in terror, as the black-robed figure cast an ominous gaze upon him.

The black-robed figure withdrew a staff from its voluminous robe. "The boy might be uncontrollable by the staff, but the gnome is ripe for the picking." Its voice was raspy, like metal rubbing against metal and an edge of cruelty in its voice.

The tone sent shivers up the young mage's spine. "Stay your course, mage. You know we are your betters. Give the boy and the gnome to us, and I promise no harm will come to you or your friends."

"He is not a lycanthrope. So, you're the one who needs to recognize their betters and leave before my friends and I kill all of you. Now stand..."

Auorak watched in horror as Nephrym screamed and writhed in pain. His limbs were elongating and twisting, his skin contorting as he thrashed about, desperately trying to free himself from whatever unseen force was causing this agony.

Val stood stock-still a few feet away from the scene, his gaze locked on the black-robed figure across from him. Beads of sweat ran down Val's face, and Auorak could tell he was engaged in a fierce battle within himself. He had seen first-hand Val's formidable skills when it came to combat; the thought of having to face him as an enemy made Auorak shiver with fear. He truly hoped that what Val had said was true and the staff could not take control of him.

Before Val's eyes, Nephrym shuddered and began to morph. His body contorted and bones cracked as his human form twisted into that of a bipedal wolf, fur erupting from his flesh in all directions.

Val stood, petrified with fear, trying to keep control over his own actions while desperately wishing he could do something for Nephrym during what was his first ever shift. He didn't know how he was going to manage it, but he had to save him; the taste of happiness he had finally experienced for the first time in his life and refused to let slip away, even if it meant sacrificing himself.

"Wolfy! Does the wee fluff ball have your healing?" Yelled Barnabiz as he stormed across the room. Barnabiz swung his massive maul, knocking the wee werewolf into the adjacent wall with a thud. "There, problem solved. You may have been controlling the wee wolf. But you aren't controlling shit for a few minutes. Maybe an hour. I did underestimate the swing a tad."

A searing fury engulfed Val's body like an inferno. He could feel the hatred coursing through his veins, shaking his core. His eyes narrowed as the party of revelers stood wide-eyed at the sight before them. A ten-foot-tall humanoid werewolf in full regalia, brandishing

119

two swords that glinted with a menacing gleam.

Val had morphed into something almost unrecognizable in its darkness and terror. Though the party had all seen Val shift before, there was something different this time.

"Bloody fucking hell. We have officially pissed off the puppy." Barnabiz reDraks as he backed away slowly. Secretly hoping young Val still thought of them as friends and went after the black-robed mage.

"It's the black-robed mage's fault, Val. He made us do it. Nephrym will be fine. He might have a headache. Ok, he is definitely going to have a headache for a bit. But hey, you can always pole the Dragonborn. I mean, bestiality is sorta your thing, right?" Lupine awkwardly sputtered out as he, too, backed away.

Val sprinted up to the black-robed mage. The elf looked up from his incantations and raised his staff of control. Young Val spun and swung his swords at the mage; one blade shattered the elf's skull, while another cut a second wizard in half as though he were made of cheese instead of flesh. Val's blades hit the staff of control and destroyed it, and the blast knocked young Val back a good ten feet, but he never once lost his balance or footing.

"Rouse the furry gods' forsaken gnome! Do it now!" Drak bellowed, sprinting towards the lifeless body of Nephrym. He had never yearned for Nephrym's shrill, annoying voice more than at that moment. "Wake him up so he calls off his dog!" Suddenly, a bloodcurdling howl pierced through the stillness and echoed in their ears like a warning from hell.

Out of nowhere, Barnabiz whipped it out and proceeded to urinate all over Nephrym. The gnome began to stir. The pungent odor of ogre piss will apparently wake up any living creature and probably some which are not.

"What is that gods' forsaken smell?" Nephrym groaned as he slowly woke up. Each groan was achy and painful. His tongue felt thick, his throat dry. He can see two of everything; the second image of the ogre became smaller and smaller until it finally vanished. "Why am I seeing triple? Everything is blurry?" He asked himself, even though he had no answer to this question.

The party watched in horror as Val leaped at Nephrym, his werewolf form making it impossible to tell if he was going to be saved or ripped apart. They all knew that the black mage had done something to him, but none of them could have guessed just how powerful Val really was.

As Val held Nephrym in his arms, they could only hope and pray that he would not succumb to the power of the demon inside him. But what they did not know was that during their battle for control, it was not just Val's mind that was being fought over — it was his soul.

The demon within wanted nothing more than to take full control, fulfill its prophecy and bring chaos and destruction wherever it went. All this while Barnabiz yelled "FOUR!" and swung his massive maul at the blue-robed mage's head, sending bits of flesh flying everywhere.

"Damn, elves!" Barnabiz spat. "May you all be food for the maggots!"

As their comrades fell in the heat of battle, the remaining mages wasted no time. With a flick of their wrists and a burst of energy, they disappeared from the bloody battlefield - teleporting away from what would surely have been their deaths.

The air crackled with magic as they vanished, leaving behind only the echo of their movements and the scent of burnt ozone hanging in the air.

The party noticed a hole knocked in the wall. Exposed, what appeared to be a room beyond it. A well-lit room gleaming and abandoned, almost begging to be explored. Inside, they could see all sorts of treasures. Everything from bejeweled weaponry to tomes and scrolls. This had to be where the relics they were searching for were.

"Now we're talking. Come to Papa!" Lupine plowed through the hole and landed on his knees in the room. All that could be heard was the tiny goblin wailing as he dove into piles of gold coins and made snowy angel imprints in the treasure.

Auorak slowly walked towards the newly made hole in the wall, a grin on his lips and an eagle eye inspecting every brick for a hidden trap. His voice was calm as he turned to his companion. "Next time you decide to jump through a mysterious hole, it would be wise to check for traps first. I'd hate for you to fall victim to your own recklessness and have me turn your corpse into a zombie slave for the ogre."

"So long as you command me to slit your mage throat in your sleep, I am good with it, actually."

After what felt like hours, the party all managed to climb through the hole in the wall. Having to make the hole much bigger to be an ogre size hole. The room, however, was quite large.

Much larger, in fact, than it looked through the small hole in the wall. It was as if it went on forever, gold coins and statues everywhere.

"Hold the fuck on!" Drak reDraks as he raised his arms, signaling the group to stop. "Something is not right here. This looks and awful lot like a dragon hoard. And being a part dragon, I know dragon hoards. This is a dragon hoard. We do not want any part of a dragon's hoard."

Drak

"So, what is it you're trying to tell us?" Asked Lupine.

"Well, first off. It is a fucking dragon hoard! Second, and we do not want to steal from a fucking dragon."

"First off, your eminence, I do not see any dragon. And second, if we do not get caught by the dragon, it will never know."

Lupine explained as he tried to justify himself to Drak and the party. He had already stuffed a couple of golden goblets and coins into his rucksack.

"The dragon always knows. It will track us down one by one until every last gold coin is accounted for. We need to leave now." Everyone can tell Drak is worried even though they all tried to act as if they did not. Everyone felt uneasiness and fear rising.

Chapter 7

I Told You It Was a Fucking Dragon Horde

The chatter in the room slowly died as a low, guttural growl emerged from the shadows of the far west wall. The air seemed to thicken and drop several degrees as a black mist began to slowly fan out into the center of the room.

All eyes were upon it, fingers trembling as the mist drifted and curled like a wave before them. Out of its depths stepped a child, no more than eight or nine years old. The child's eyes were glazed over, and his clothes were tattered.

"May the gods have mercy on us! What abomination is this? What foul and unholy thing is happening before our very eyes?" Auorak gaped in horror as he and the rest of his band slowly began to back away, unable to look away from whatever the boy was shambling closer and closer toward them. The air itself around them seemed to congeal with terror, like a thick, heavy fog.

"What exactly does it…" Lupine began to ask, but his voice was cut off by a small, sinister laugh. He turned to see an eerie figure in the corner of the room, barely visible in the darkness.

As if to answer his question, the young boy stepped forward into the light and addressed them. "Hello! My name is Dimitri. Are you here to take me home? I've been all alone for so long now, and I'm dying for somebody to take me home." The chill that ran down Lupine's spine told him all he needed to know. This child wasn't seeking friendship - he had something far more sinister in store.

Dimitri

"What is it with us and creepy little buggers? First, we have Baron Von Fairywolf, now this little bastard." Barnabiz looks the boy up and down. Trying to figure out exactly how the young boy is going to be a pain in the party's ass. "I vote we adopt a no creepy little buggers clause. We see em' and we kill em'. Much safer."

"Nobody else is down here with you, are they?" Navine pleaded as she cautiously stepped closer to the child. "What kind of person would leave a poor soul in this dangerous ruin?"

Navine stared in awe as the child slowly morphed into a sinister mist. In a split second, it devoured her into its depths, yet she did not go quietly. The haunting screams of terror echoed through the darkness until they were abruptly silenced by an unseen force. As the mists slowly dispersed, red blood trickled down from where Navine had stood, and all that remained was an eerie chill in the stale air and a bloodstain upon the floor of the room.

"And just for your information, priest, I am over nine hundred years old. And you are correct about one thing: this is indeed a dragon hoard."

"I told you, bastards! And now the goblin and Navine have already pissed it off, and now we are all so fucked!" Drak yells in disgust as he draws his weapon for what he knows is going to be a no-win battle.

All of a sudden, almost as quickly as the mist had started swirling around Navine, it transformed once again back into the young lad. Navine, nowhere to be seen. No trace whatsoever. It was as if she was never there at all. This was unlike anything the party had ever experienced. What maniacal and evil forces could be behind this?

"This little bastard has to pay!" Nephrym stormed ahead, his face twisted with rage and hurt. With daggers raised, he vowed to avenge the death of his beloved companion. But in the depths of his heart, a small voice whispered doubt. Did his friend really perish, or was something else at work? He was determined to get answers but apprehensive of the road that lay ahead. The thoughts of what was to come lay heavy upon him.

Val'Rak reached out and grabbed Nephrym by the back of the neck, his grip firm but gentle. "This isn't a fight we can win," he said grimly into Nephrym's ear. "We need to honor our dead, lick our wounds and be thankful that we still have each other." Despite the direness of the situation, Val'Rak held Nephrym close in a tight embrace. "I won't let you go," he vowed. "Not like this."

The young lad once again turned into a dark black mist and moved across the room.

"Why is everyone so sad?" the young lad materializing again from the black mist as quickly as he had disappeared.

"You just killed my friend!" Nephrym shouted, his eyes red and filled with rage. He looked at the creature before him and felt a wave of sadness wash over him. He wanted revenge for what it had done, but he also couldn't help but feel pity all at the same time for the tiny thing in front of him.

The party did not know that little Dimitri, most definitely a dragon, was an unholy terror of the greatest proportions. Tuned to destroy and kill, he had been bred to be a weapon. And a weapon he was indeed.

The only one of his kind, he was the hybrid, unholy and dark-magic twisted offspring of a black dragon and an ancient vampire. His bloodline leaned more toward the vampire than the dragon sides of his genetics. That is why when his vampire nature kicked in, it froze him as a nine-year-old child with a temperament that would make any parent cringe with fear. Yet, with the destructive power of an ancient vampire and an ancient black dragon combined.

"We really need to get right with the gods. I mean, we gotta be like cursed by them or some shit." Mutters Barnabiz as he slowly and discreetly grabs the pommel of his massive great maul. "I mean, we cannot really just be this damn unlucky, can we?"

"The gods had no part in this," Drak informs Barnabiz. "At least not any god that listens to any prayers we speak." He grinds his teeth together and mumbles curse words that almost make the ogre blush.

Readying his battle hammer, he prepares himself for a fight.

Dimitri let out a loud sob as he fell to the floor, his hands covering his face. His shoulders heaved up and down with each breath as he spoke. "I am sorry about your friend. But she frightened me. And I had been so, so hungry. I hadn't eaten in months, so I couldn't control myself." He shook his head sadly and continued to cry with his arms curled protectively around himself.

"How does this sort of abomination even happen?" Auorak asks Drak as they both try to ascertain this situation.

"Just like I said before, this is the work of some dark and evil magic."

"You know you can come with us. We are all strange and unique, just like you," Val'Rak tells Dimitri while still fully in human mode.

"Show me," says Dimitri, his voice filled with curiosity. Val'Rak smiles and shifts into full-blown werewolf mode. His body morphs as the muscles underneath his skin ripple outward until he is covered with medium-length coal-black fur, and sharp claws protrude from his fingers and toes. Red eyes focus on the man before him as fangs extend from his mouth.

Lupine's eyes widened as he watched the transformation, marveling at the speed with which the man's body blurred and shifted into that of a large werewolf. He shook his head in disbelief, mouth agape. "Holy shit! How can he change that fast? Zero to wolf in like two seconds!" Having never really paid attention to the previous transformations.

Val'Rak stepped forward, a massive figure in the dark. Dimitri didn't move at first, but as Val'Rak came closer, the boy allowed himself to relax and slumped to the ground. Everyone in the party glanced around nervously, unsure of what would happen next. This was unlike anything they had ever experienced before.

Lupine spoke in a gentle voice, his hands up in the air as if to show he meant no harm. He was careful to keep all of his movements slow and steady as he met the eyes of the mysterious creature before him. "Look," he said. "There's no need for anyone or anything to get hurt here. Let's be friends, okay?"

"So, I am a thing! A thing! You all think I am a monster! I'll show you a monster!" Lupine's eyes widened in terror as the child began to transform before him. His skinny frame grew and stretched until it was unrecognizable. Dark leathery wings shot out from his back, and giant horns spiraled around his head.

With one loud roar, the newly formed black dragon reared up in front of Lupine, its razor-sharp claws scratching and gnashing at the air. Its yellow eyes glowed with fury as it lunged forward and clamped its jaws around Lupine's midsection. Putrid green acidic flames licked around Lupine's body as the dragon sunk its teeth into him, and acidic saliva dripped onto the wounds, burning deep into his flesh. He let out a blood-curdling scream.

"I'm too young to die! Please don't eat me!" Lupine pleaded with the huge dragon.

The beast stands on all fours and wraps its sinewy, clawed hand around Lupine. It raises its head up high as if to make itself more imposing. Its chest heaves in great, deep breaths of air; it is ready to pounce at the first opportunity.

Giving them a look that is unmistakable: I am starving, and you are all for dinner. Just then, Val'Rak leaps high into the air and lands, standing upright atop the dragon's back. His two swords plunge down through the scales and cleave deep into the muscles of the beast's shoulders. The dragon lets out a wail of pain that would rival that of a banshee.

Dimitri's menacing bellow echoed throughout the dark chamber as he grabbed Val'Rak and hurled him across the room. The beast licked its lips in anticipation of the delightful pleasures it would soon savor.

Lupine trembled in fear, knowing his life was coming to an end. But before Dimitri could deliver the final blow, Val'Rak suddenly sprung to action, sinking his teeth deep into the beast's throat.

The dragon screamed out in agony as Val'Rak continued his relentless assault. Dark ichor sprayed from its wound like a fountain of death. Its body quivered and writhed until, finally, it lay still on the cold stone floor. Not even a single breath escaped its mangled corpse.

The rest of the party stared in awe at what they had witnessed, each of them pondering if such horrific power could ever be wielded for good. The dragon's corpse lay lifeless on the cold stone floor.

Drak found himself left in a daze of confusion, his mouth agape in utter disbelief. He wasn't sure what had just happened. Fear and uncertainty crept into his being, and he felt a wave of panic wash over him as he stammered, "Oh my God...what the hell?".

A chill descended upon the group as Barnabiz examined the dragon's lifeless body, its empty eye sockets seeming to peer into their souls. "Well, I think the wretched little fiend boy consumed, violated, or murdered Navine in some way," he declared, prodding its head with his boot. "Whatever it is, I can assure you that it is most certainly deceased." An eerie stillness hung in the air.

"Holy hell, think you could have waited any longer? I thought sure I was getting eaten by whatever the hell that thing was." Lupine gasps as he drags himself from under the small dragon's now dead and limp body.

Val'Rak's furry face was creased with worry as he watched Nephrym. His white claws dug into the ground, his fur standing on end in anticipation of the transformation. As Val shifted from wolf to man, he stumbled forward and embraced him tightly, almost squeezing the air out of Nephrym's lungs.

"Note to self: never threaten the gnome when he has his puppy around," Barnabiz smirked as he wiped the dragon's blood and entrails from himself. "It seems that would not go to fucking well for the lot of us."

Nephrym thrashed in Val'Rak's grip, his eyes wide with terror. "Put me down! I can't breathe!" he yelled. He looked at the creature with confusion, desperate to understand what it was - a boy? A vampire? A dragon? His heart pounded as he waited for an answer that never came.

"Are you alright? Did anything happen to you?" Val'Rak felt a chill of fear run through him as he thought of Nephrym being injured in any way. He had done so much to make it this far and was not willing to let anything come between him and his dreams. But at the same time, his heart ached with worry, knowing that he could not protect Nephrym from everything.

Lupine's face was streaked with dirt and sweat, and he shook with anger as he yelled at them like two kids.

"Hello, I was almost eaten by a damn whatchamacallit dragon thingy!!" His hands balled into fists as he remembered the horror of seeing one of his friends devoured by an alien shapeshifter and almost getting eaten himself. He had watched in disbelief as it transformed into a dragon, and if not for Val'Rak's quick reflexes, he, too, would have been consumed. Storming away from the pair, Lupine fought to mask the fear that threatened to overwhelm him.

Drak's voice thundered throughout the room, each word crushing his companions with its unbridled power. "Are you truly as cold and unforgiving as you pretend? We could ALL have been killed by your reckless actions, you foolish little brat! Give us this one chance to celebrate what we still have before it is too late. Yet, here in the Land of Dodd, death may be the only outcome... or WORSE!" His words echoed ominously around them all, a reminder of the horrors they must face if they did not unite.

Lupine's face twisted into an apologetic grimace, and he scratched the back of his neck in embarrassment. He had been trying to lighten the mood with a little humor, hoping to quell any emotion that threatened to overpower him. But as soon as the words left his lips, he wished he could take them back. His gaze shifted away from everyone else in the room, not wanting to bear witness to their reactions—the anger or disappointment—he was so used to seeing.

But sometimes laughter was all there was left for him to use, even if it was at someone else's expense. "Well, at least now you can say you have been fellated by a dragon, a vampire and a young boy all at once. They will either be impressed and buy you a drink just to hear the story or lock you up and throw away the key. Either way, they are gonna think you're a sick little bastard." Chuckled Barnabiz as he, too tried to lighten up the mood.

Val'Rak's eyes scanned the hoard warily as if searching for any sign of life. Satisfied, he let out a deep sigh and began to remove his armor and pack all his gear onto the ground. He took a seat on a pile of gold coins with a satisfied grunt and pointed around at the dragon's hoard. "I think we can rest here safely," he said. "Nothing would dare approach this place. Call us all crazy or mad, but I think this is our best choice."

"Are you implying we're mad, wolfy?" Barnabiz drawled. Drak laughed mirthlessly as he too, started removing his garments. "Madness doesn't even begin to describe us. Our insanity is so profound that even people who are considered 'crazy' keep their distance from us. Death follows us like a moth drawn to light, and we laugh in its face. We all know that no matter what happens, whether we live or die, we must stay on the path we have chosen. Each of us has come to terms with our mortality. Have you?"

Chapter 8
Farther Into the Gaping Maw of Hell, You Say

Time had long since lost its relevance in the ancient ruins; the group had nc idea whether it was day or night. Exhaustion had set in, and everyone was desperate to get some rest, even if it meant sleeping in the same chamber as the dead dragon that had killed their friend. It seemed like an absurdly bad idea, but after days of never getting five minutes of sleep, any hope for a few hours of uninterrupted slumber was worth any price.

Barnabiz peered down at the tiny, sleeping goblin with a smirk. He felt an urge to pull a prank on him but knew that he was too exhausted to think of something.

Instead, he simply shook his head and mumbled, "Awww, look at that. Little goblin shit for brains is already passed out." Disheartened, he trudged across the room of golden coins and collapsed onto one of the smaller piles, trying his hardest to relax.

Val'Rak grabbed Nephrym's chin in his hand, tilting his head up and forcing him to look into his intense gaze.

"You must rest now, Nephrym. These next few weeks will take a toll on your body and soul. Promise me that you will never forget that I love you, no matter what may come." Val'Rak's words echoed with meaning as he caressed the back of Nephrym's neck tenderly.

His heart raced as he felt the menacingly familiar presence of the demon lurking in his mind. He desperately fought against its insidious and beguiling whispers, trying to cling on to what remained of his sanity.

The inner battle seemed pointless as the demon's power became more and more dominant. It was relentless in its promises of solace and liberation if only he could succumb to its will for a mere second. Val'Rak knew these were nothing but lies; there was no way out, only an inevitable descent into darkness and ruin if he surrendered even an inch. With a Herculean effort, he continued to resist, knowing that any hint of distraction would be fatal.

Val watched as exhaustion won out, and the whole group fell asleep. Nephrym lay on his side, one arm draped across his chest and the other tucked beneath his head. His breathing was steady, almost peaceful. In stark contrast to him, the ogre snored loudly enough that Val was surprised anyone slept at all. He felt a strange mix of wonder and envy as he studied each of her companions in turn.

Val watched Nephrym sleep, feeling a warmth and sense of peace that was unfamiliar to him. People actually cared about him for who he was - not his father's wealth or power or his potential to become something greater one day. In this moment all Val wanted was to be accepted and loved by those around him, even if it was fleeting.

Val begins to hear a sinister voice whisper in his mind from the dark abyss of his subconscious.

"Let us put an end to them all, my child. I will help you do extraordinary things. Free yourself from these wretched mortals and ascend to your true destiny." The voice speaks with malicious intent, beckoning Val to give in to its tempting offer.

Val was assaulted by the overwhelming presence of the demon, begging and pleading for control. He felt its raw energy coursing through his veins, promising strength and power beyond belief - no one would ever harm him or even have the courage to try; Nephrym would be safe from any harm. His mind warred against the pressure, screaming 'NO!' as he felt the demon's grasp tighten around his soul.

Val knew this battle was his alone to fight, that if he were to unleash the terror inside him, it could lead him down a path of destruction like last time when he murdered an entire village before finally being able to take back control. Could he be strong enough to beat it this time?

Barnabiz groaned as he was pulled from his sleep, the sound of wailing like nails on a chalkboard. He rubbed his bleary eyes and muttered under his breath, "What's all that racket? Some of us are trying to get some shut-eye!" His gaze narrowed as he glared at the source of the noise. "Noisy little tick," he spat.

Lupine leaned in close to Nephrym, his lips pursed and a mischievous glint in his eye.

"Awwh. Did somebody have a bad dream?" His hand reached out to pinch the gnome's cheek, only to be met with swift resistance as Nephrym's tiny palm connected with him mid-air.

Lupine was indeed correct, to some extent. For Nephrym, it wasn't a dream but a vision of things to come - one of the few good perks of having a demonic entity growing inside of him. His mind's eye brought him memories that were so vivid he could feel them as if they were in the present moment. He could smell the metallic scent of blood in the air; he could hear screams that sent ice coursing through his veins. But most terrifying of all, he could feel the fear radiating from future events and knew beyond any doubt that these were visions of what may come to pass.

Nephrym's voice was trembling as he spoke to Val. "I don't know if I can handle this, Val. The changes that are happening…they're overwhelming." Tears started to well up in his eyes. "And these dreams or visions…are they the future? Is this what we're supposed to become?" Val looked at Nephrym with a mixture of fear and worry. She knew the stakes were high, but she had no idea how to reassure him.

"Nephrym," she began hesitantly. "We'll make it through this together."

"But will we make it out intact?" Nephrym's voice rose with desperation.

"Will we still be ourselves when all is said and done?" Val's heart felt like it was breaking as she realized the severity of their situation. She took a deep breath and tried to steady her own nerves before answering, "I don't have an answer for that yet. But I promise you one thing...I won't stop fighting until we're safe." The silence hung heavily between them for a moment before Nephrym finally responded quietly, "Okay." But Val could see the uncertainty in his eyes.

Val uttered the words, "Everything is going to be fine," with a slight hint of uncertainty in his voice. Despite trying to reassure himself, he had countless questions that he was too afraid to ask. He knew deep inside that there was no guarantee that things would turn out alright, but he chose to remain optimistic and look forward to a brighter future.

"I can hear our child speaking to me when I sleep. He thinks I am going to die when he is born. I have seen his birth. I know that I will not survive it. How could anyone survive that? Yet, I already love our child and would not stop this if I could. I am haunted with a fear something is going to happen."

Val's heart ached as he made the ultimate sacrifice for his beloved.

Despite knowing that this would unleash a world of unknown horrors, Val could not leave Nephrym to die. He had to take matters into his own hands and make a deal with the demon - giving up control in order to save his loved one and child. But still, what price was he going to pay? How much harm would come as a result of his actions? The only thing that was certain was that Nephrym would be safe.

Drak snarled at Nephrym, his patience fraying. "You can't be serious," he spat. "Do you know what this will do to you? Death and terror await your every step with that abomination in tow. Don't you understand? The gods have revealed their judgment to me - we must act now! We're your friends, don't you remember? Please!" His words echoed in the darkness, a haunting reminder of the fate awaiting Nephrym.

The words shook Nephrym to his core. He felt tears in his eyes, unable to control his sobbing. His friends surrounded him with any comfort they could offer, yet he still felt like a sinking ship in a desolate sea. Was this really what was being asked of him? The thought seemed impossible, and he felt helpless, unable to decide what would be right.

Lupine put his hand on his friend's shoulder, trying to comfort him. He knew his friend was overwhelmed and struggling to figure out what to do next.

"Look," he said in a soothing voice. "We don't have to decide now. We still have at least another week or two down here until we can find whatever this mysterious thing Retsnimle is after. Then we can get out of here and work it all out afterward."

Val's face drooped with annoyance at the suggestion that Nephrym or their son were in danger. He failed to recognize the true concern in their friends' eyes as they spoke. "Yes, let us do just that. And if any of you try to harm Nephrym or our son, you will suffer a fate from which you will beg for death every day."

Lupine growled at Val. "Hurt my friend, dog breath. I will end you. I will gut you like a fish. Understand?" Lupine hoped Val would realize how much he did care for his friend.

The group of friends huddled around Nephrym and Val, exchanging warm glances and gentle pats on the shoulder in silent support. Despite only knowing the lad for a brief period, they had grown close and developed an odd familial bond.

The fate of the Land of Dodd hung precariously in the balance like a teetering scale, and it was up to them to decide which direction it would tip.

Bryan Kurt Dodd

Chapter 9
The Old Ogre Cookbook

The air was thick with a clammy chill, the walls slick with moisture, and their breaths rose in faint clouds, frosting in the cold. The adventurers had spent two more days weaving through the narrow tunnels of the ancient elven dwelling, anxiety growing with each step deeper into its depths. Every faint rustle or distant creak jolted them, making it nearly impossible to hear anything over their own racing hearts.

Auorak swept the torch around the room, casting dancing shadows that stretched and shrank in every corner. He wanted to remain hopeful, but an unnerving stillness seemed to press in from all sides. The place had a weight of silence about it, an ominous energy that prickled at the back of his mind, urging him to turn back before it was too late.

Exhaustion crept up on them like a thief in the night. Lupine dropped his pack to the ground, sinking down with a long, weary sigh as if relieved to find even a moment's rest. He glanced around, his expression one of wary disbelief. "It's like something has cleared everything out," he murmured. "I think it's time for a break."

"You're right," Auorak replied, setting down his gear with a thud. As he shifted his foot, it caught on a subtle ridge in the carved stone floor, revealing ancient, glowing runes inscribed beneath the dust. He knelt, squinting to make out the details.

Lupine raised an eyebrow, looking over. "I am? Right about what?"

"About something frightening everything away. There's a power here, close and powerful, like nothing we've felt before. I can sense it—magic woven through every stone and shadow, everywhere and nowhere at once." Auorak ran his hand along the etched floor, feeling a pulse of ancient elven magic stir within him. "Whatever this is, it wants Nephrym... and Val."

Val's eyes flickered with fear as he spoke, his voice barely a whisper. He could feel the lich's pull—an ancient call seeping through his staff, urging him toward an inevitable, terrifying fate. He struggled against it, but the more he resisted, the stronger the pull became, like a siren song drawing him closer to oblivion.

Nephrym laid his gear on the floor with a heavy sigh, the weight of their quest pressing upon him. They both knew the stakes if Val yielded to the lich's dark power, yet they had no choice but to press on. Somewhere, the lich waited, intent on unleashing a demon upon the Land of Dodd.

Drak's eyes went wide, his mouth falling open in shock. "A lich? You're serious?" His mind raced as the gravity of their situation sank in—they were up against an undead creature, one that wielded ancient, lethal magic beyond any of their skills. A thousand doubts flooded his mind: why hadn't they been warned of this? Could they really survive this? He wished they could turn back, yet he knew it was far too late.

Barnabiz grinned, patting his belly. "After we kill it, I'll make a big pot of lich bone stew. Old ogre delicacy—you'll love it." He leaned confidently against his massive great maul, giving a wink.

Drak guffawed, doubling over with laughter as he set down his equipment. "All these old-fashioned ogre recipes! Careful, Barnabiz—don't let folks mistake you for a chef instead of a bard!"

But Auorak's face had drained of color. He scanned the room again, taking in the complex sigils carved into the walls and floor. His hands trembled as he gestured toward the intricate designs, their meanings hidden and yet, he feared, deadly clear.

"Guys, I'm not so sure this is a good place to... well, to do anything," he said, his voice wavering slightly. "This entire room is one massive summoning circle. I've never seen one this big—it would take at least a dozen skilled mages if not more, to sustain a circle of this magnitude."

Drak's heart thundered as he stared down at the ancient runes, hardly able to believe anyone would dare call upon forces so powerful. A shiver crawled up his spine as he muttered a desperate prayer to the gods, pleading for their protection. He could only imagine the horrors that might have been conjured—and unleashed— in this very place.

Auorak's eyes darted around the chamber, taking in strange symbols etched into the stone. The symbols seemed to twist and coil, entwined with a purpose that made his stomach turn.

Stepping closer, he examined them, and his breath caught in his throat: they were spell circles meant for demonic summoning. His face drained of color as he took in the full weight of the room. An invisible wave of terror pressed in, a shadow of suffering and fear that clung to the walls, whispering of horrors long past but never truly gone.

The tales of the elves' demise flooded his mind—chilling stories of summoning rituals gone horrifically wrong. It was said that the elves had tried to control forces beyond their power, unleashing demonic entities too powerful to bind. The Land of Dodd had been plunged into chaos, entire cities reduced to ruins, as the elves fell one by one to the evil they had unleashed. Now, only a handful of their kind remained, scattered and hidden, their numbers fading from the land.

Val gazed around the room, his eyes drawn to the fine, delicate sculptures lining the walls and floors. "I've never seen an elf before until all of this," he murmured, running a finger along the curves of a finely crafted figure, the elegance of the work a haunting reminder of what had been lost.

Barnabiz's voice quivered with rage; each word spat with venom. His eyes blazed, his veins bulging, and he jabbed a finger in the air. "They're nothing but foul and corrupt!" he snarled, his voice trembling with a barely restrained fury. "Corrupting everything they touch with their vile magic!" The others watched in stunned silence, taken aback by the intensity of Barnabiz's anger.

Memories surged up within Barnabiz, fueling his hatred. He remembered the lashes of the elves' whips, the sting of wounds long scarred over, and the sight of his parents collapsing under their cruel demands. He had been just a small ogre whelp when he'd managed to escape, the pain and humiliation carved deep into his bones. From that day forward, he had vowed to rid the Land of Dodd of the elvish menace that haunted it. Barnabiz was unique in their group—he had seen a true-blooded elf with his own eyes, though now only a few remained, hiding their identities and avoiding detection.

Lupine's voice broke the silence, daring to ask the question on everyone's mind. "Exactly how old are you?" he asked, his tone tinged with curiosity and caution.

Barnabiz lunged forward, his face turning a mottled red. "Old enough—I may very well have eaten your grandparents," he growled, voice echoing off the stone walls. "You pig-eared little runt!" He seemed to swell with rage at the audacity of the question, his entire frame shaking.

Lupine could barely contain his laughter, clutching his sides as he doubled over. "Old ogre delicacy!" he wheezed, his laughter echoing through the tense silence.

Barnabiz's eyes gleamed with dark amusement, a cruel smile twisting his lips as he hoisted his pack higher. He stepped to the edge of the platform, his gaze cold as he took the first few steps into their descent. "Laugh it up," he called over his shoulder. "But remember, if we start starving in this gods-forsaken place, you're the first I'll be eating."

The group pressed on, their progress slow and wary. The air thickened, a sulfurous stench burning their nostrils and stinging their eyes. A lingering chill seeped into their bones, each breath rising as mist into the frigid air. Time felt distorted as if it were stretching and folding in on itself as they trudged forward, inching closer to something unknown—and unknowingly toward a fate that awaited in the depths.

Ahead, an ominous light filtered through the doorway, its flickering glow casting twisted shadows that seemed to crawl closer, beckoning them into the depths.

Strange shapes flitted in the darkness beyond, their outlines shifting, forming, and dissolving with each heartbeat, yet a deadly silence hung in the air—a silence so absolute it swallowed even the sound of their breaths. Hearts thundered in their chests as they moved forward, every step measured, every movement cautious, edging toward the unknown.

Drak's gaze drifted to the doorframe, and his eyes widened. Faint glimmers of arcane symbols wound around the stone, interlocking in a maze of intricate patterns that seemed to pulse with dark energy. He instinctively stepped back, murmuring, "By the gods, what foul magic are we witnessing?" His words were barely above a whisper, yet they echoed, lost in the stifling silence.

As the group pressed through the threshold, they halted, horror spreading over their faces. In the center of the room stood a massive granite altar, dark and foreboding, its surface slick with layers of dried, congealed blood that caught the faint light, casting a sickly sheen.

Atop it lay the remains of a body—or rather, what was left of one. The flesh had been peeled back in ribbons, exposing organs that spilled over the edge and pooled onto the floor, remnants of some unspeakable ritual.

The ancient air felt thick with dread, crackling with a tension that gripped each of them like a vice. Even the walls seemed to whisper, the faint echoes of a language lost to time, as if the stones themselves recoiled from the blasphemous scene.

Ever so slowly, the weight of realization pressed upon them—this was no ordinary place, no ordinary horror. By the gods, what had they just walked in on?

Bryan Kurt Dodd

Chapter 10

Son Of A Lich

Val's lip quivered as he stepped closer to the cold, macabre altar, his heart sinking with each step. A single tear traced a slow path down his cheek as he reached out, his trembling fingers brushing over the corpse's forehead. His hand lingered there, tracing the disfigured features, and an icy chill surged through him as recognition hit—a devastating wave of horror. The lifeless figure lying before him was none other than his own brother.

The truth crashed over him like a torrent, knocking the breath from his lungs. His brother—the one person who had always been there, his steadfast anchor in a world filled with chaos—was gone, forever lost to the darkness that had claimed him.

A strangled cry tore from Val's throat, echoing off the stone walls, drowning out all other sounds as it reverberated in the hollow chamber.

He sank to his knees, fists pounding the ground as his voice broke through the silence, raw with grief. "I know him! I know this man! He is my brother!" Tears flowed freely now, streaming down his face as he slumped forward, his body wracked with sobs.

Nephrym stepped forward, extending a comforting hand and placing it gently on Val's shoulder. He could feel the weight of his friend's sorrow as if it were his own.

Though Nephrym had never known the depth of a brotherly bond like Val's, his heart ached in sympathy, sharing in the profound sadness that filled the room. A tear slipped down his own cheek—not only for Val's pain but for the emptiness he himself felt at never having experienced such a bond.

Drak, silent until now, knelt beside them, his voice soft yet laced with a dark promise. "We will avenge these heinous crimes," he said, his gaze fixed on the disfigured form of Val's brother. "Your revenge will be exacted with a fury and cruelty a thousand times more vicious than what was done to him. Let there be no doubt—justice will be served."

Val's brother

Lupine stood speechless, his mouth slightly open, his eyes wide and transfixed on the ghastly sight before him. The raw reality of what lay before him seeped in like poison, gnawing at his sanity. His mind scrambled to comprehend the scene, but every attempt felt futile, slipping through his grasp.

A creeping sense of dread took hold, sinking its claws deep within him, and he felt the weight of being completely out of his depth. All his training, all his bravado—it seemed laughably small against the enormity of the horror before him.

Beside him, Auorak stumbled back, nearly tripping over his own feet. He gasped, his breath shallow, as his eyes traveled across the blood-drenched altar and the mangled body upon it. The remains were scattered—bits of flesh and cloth torn asunder, littered around the altar like pieces of a grisly jigsaw puzzle.

The sharp, acrid smell of burnt hair and seared metal hung heavy in the air, stinging his nose and burning his throat. He could almost feel the residue of agony in the very stones, as though they had absorbed the suffering that had taken place within these walls.

He whispered, barely audible, his voice a fragile thread of horror. "What foul magic did this? What kind of creature could be so cruel?"

Val, however, was beyond words. His fists clenched so tightly that his knuckles cracked like thunder, reverberating in the heavy silence. His chest heaved with rage that rolled inside him like a storm, each surge more violent than the last. His once gentle eyes had turned into narrowed slits, dark and furious, glinting with a fire that threatened to consume him. A low growl rumbled from deep within his chest, a sound more beast than man.

"That bastard lich wizard did this," he spat, his voice thick with venom. "He tried to bond my brother's soul with that of a demon." His lips twisted into a snarl, his entire body quivering with the need to lash out, to destroy. "He better be careful what he wishes for because I'll show him what a real demon is capable of doing!"

As Val began to advance, Barnabiz's large hand shot out, gripping the young man's shoulders with such force that it seemed his bones might splinter under the pressure. With a near-feral growl, Barnabiz shook him, his voice a harsh snarl.

"Get ahold of yourself!" Barnabiz's voice boomed, echoing off the stone walls. "Face the facts! He's gone! Nothing you do now can bring him back." Barnabiz's face twisted with a mix of anger and sorrow, his grip tightening on Val's shoulders.

"If you let vengeance take hold of you now, you won't just lose him—you'll lose yourself too, and everyone standing here with you." His voice softened, but only just, as he added, "I know what it's like to let revenge guide you. And trust me—it'll lead you straight to ruin."

Val's breaths came in sharp gasps, his chest rising and falling with the intensity of his emotions. His gaze locked onto Barnabiz's, and for a moment, he looked like he might fight back, but the strength of the ogre's grip and the grim sincerity in his words struck him like a slap. Gradually, his shoulders sagged, his fists loosening, and the fury in his eyes dimmed, leaving a deep, hollow pain in its place.

The group stood there in silence, surrounded by death and sorrow, with the shadows watching, seeming to judge their every move. The flickering torchlight played tricks on the walls, casting monstrous shapes across the room as if echoing the torment that had been inflicted here. And somewhere in the distance, it seemed as if the very stones themselves wept for the dead, resonating with the grief of those who stood before them, awaiting the next step in their harrowing journey.

Nephrym grabbed Val's shoulders and pulled him close, speaking in a desperate whisper. "We need this, Val. We have to stay together, or else we won't make it out of here alive. Our only hope is if we stand as one, united in purpose. Do it for me, for our unborn son, for all of us," he pleaded, his voice wavering, a single tear sliding down his face. He knew the truth—without unity, survival was just a fantasy.

Lupine raised an eyebrow, casting a knowing smirk at his longtime friend. "The gnomish cock sock is right, you know. You're too important to lose. No way we can get out of this without you. It's gonna take all of us to do this, eh?" he said, giving a playful punch to Val and Nephrym's shoulders.

But even as his friends rallied around him, Val felt a dark presence seep into his mind like a venomous snake, coiling and whispering insidiously. The voice promised him power and dominance—the strength to protect those he loved. Its words were a dangerous comfort, a subtle invitation to succumb. He could feel his defenses weaken as the temptation grew stronger, urging him to give in.

Suddenly, an icy chill swept through the room, and the very air around them seemed to solidify, thickening with an oppressive dread. A gut-wrenching screech of stone against stone reverberated in the chamber, filling it with a sound that clawed at their sanity, extinguishing any remaining sense of escape.

The door slid shut, its cold finality like a prison cell locking them into this macabre realm. Darkness pressed in from every side, casting shadows that writhed like silent phantoms. It was as if they'd been sentenced to eternity in a place forsaken by light and mercy. The walls seemed to close in, a suffocating reminder of the horrors that had once unfolded within these cursed confines.

They were now prisoners, held captive by a room drenched in sinister energy. Each stone seemed to echo with the cries of lost souls, memories of innocence sacrificed for dark purposes. The overwhelming malevolence seeped into their bones, a reminder of the abominations that had stained these walls.

A maniacal cackle pierced the silence, an icy whisper that seemed to come from all directions. "Foolish mortals," it hissed. "You think you can stand against me? You are ants before a force of true darkness, a god of pure evil. Even the darkest powers bow before me."

A sound louder than thunder shook the room, the force reverberating through their very souls, filling them with a paralyzing fear. "Bow down and worship your new god!" it bellowed, each word sharper than a blade. "You pitiful creatures are nothing before me— but perhaps your broken bodies will serve a purpose yet!"

Barnabiz's rage surged like a tidal wave, fierce enough to shatter steel. His hand gripped his maul with unbreakable resolve, his face twisted with fury. "Who the hell does this clown think he is?" he snarled, his voice laced with defiance. The tension in the room grew thick as his battle cry echoed off the walls, and though death loomed, he stood undaunted. "I will not bow!" he roared, his words striking like a hammer blow. "You will bow before me when I'm done!"

Drak bellowed with a force to match the ogre's, declaring his unwavering loyalty to the Land of Dodd. His face was set like stone, his hand gripping his battle axe with lethal intent. He stood ready, braced to confront whatever darkness dared challenge them. Here was a man who had come to terms with his own mortality, willing to face death rather than surrender their land to evil.

Auorak began to chant an ancient spell, and the torches lining the walls burst into vibrant purple flames, their eerie, eldritch glow casting twisted shadows that danced across the stone. The flickering light gave the room an even more menacing aura.

"Better to see the evil we die to than to face it blindly in the darkness," he murmured ominously, his voice echoing like a spectral warning.

Lupine took a shaky step back, his eyes locked on the now-empty altar. His finger quivered, pointing toward the stained stone in a silent plea for the others to see. His breath quickened, misting in the frigid air as a chill ran down his spine.

"Guys," he whispered hoarsely, his voice nearly a whimper, "I don't wanna be the one to tell you this, but... Wolfy's brother is gone."

As the words left his lips, his gaze fell upon fresh droplets of blood splattered across the floor, a chilling reminder that their nightmare was far from over.

Val's voice rips from his throat like a ragged scream of pure hatred and vengeance. His eyes burn with blue fire as he throws back his head and unleashes a feral howl that echoes through the mountainside. He transforms into an enormous werewolf, towering above them with primal rage radiating from every inch of its fur.

"Come and get me, you wretched spellcaster!" Val bellows. "You will regret this day for all eternity."

Val felt the icy touch of evil as it snaked through his veins, paralyzing him with fear. The darkness inside spoke to him like a siren song, calling out to be released.

"That's it, my young friend," it said in a whisper that carried on the wind. "Embrace your true abilities; free me for just a moment, and I will fix everything."

Val trembled at the promise as the demon within fought to take control. "Just a moment and it will all be okay."

Val's heart raced as he thought of the risk he was taking. He had never been afraid of death, but now his fear had shifted to the safety of Nephrym and their unborn son. He clenched his fists in an effort to quell the rising anguish that threatened to overwhelm him. His courage wavered, but he steeled himself against what lay ahead for those he loved.

A deep, guttural growl rumbled in the air, and then another. A few faltered steps, then a few more. Val wobbled on landing like a puppet with its strings cut. His feet shuffled forward step by step. The demon seized control of Val before he knew what hit him.

Val's body convulsed as the demon took over, his eyes turning black as his form began to distort and change even more. It was a painful transformation as spikes burst from his shoulders, and horns sprouted from his head as his bones rearranged themselves.

As Val's senses returned to him, he could smell the stench of the crypt ghast and hear the sound of its talons scraping against the stone floor. But even with these distractions, his priority was Nephrym. Val knew that protecting Nephrym was all that mattered now, and he would stop at nothing to keep him safe.

A low growl escaped his throat as he locked eyes with the ghast, a primal urge to protect taking over his every thought. He lunged forward, claws extended, aiming straight for the creature's neck.

The ghast let out a piercing shriek, its wings flapping frantically as it tried to fend off Val's ferocious attack. But Val was relentless, driven by an animalistic fury that allowed him to easily overpower the   ghast. With one swift motion, he tore off one of its wings, causing it to plummet to the ground. But it wasn't over yet.

Val could sense more danger looming ahead, and he knew that he needed to keep moving if he wanted to ensure Nephrym's safety. With a snarl still fixed on his lips, Val began moving forward once again, determined to face whatever came next head-on.

Lupine felt the weight of terror tighten his chest as he stumbled backward into the wall. His eyes wide and disbelieving, he heard himself whisper with a trembling voice, "What... what in God's name is that?! Nephrym, what... is... that?!"

Val's swords clashed against the crypt ghast with enough force to shake the foundations of the earth. Sparks flew from every impact, and each movement exploded with ferocity as they fought for their lives. The atmosphere was thick with tension as if even the air itself knew that only one would survive this showdown.

When Val stood victorious over his foe, he knew that in order to protect those dearest to him, he had to hunt down and confront whoever sent this beast against them.

As Val fought the crypt ghast, he could feel the demon within him urging him on. He knew that he was stronger with the demon's influence, but at what cost? He had to protect Nephrym and their unborn son from the ghast's clutches, but he couldn't let the demon take over completely.

The ghast was quick and nimble, dodging Val's attacks with ease.

Its claws scraped across Val's chest, leaving deep gashes that oozed blood. But Val didn't falter. He had to keep fighting. The fate of Nephrym and their son hung in the balance.

Val saw an opening and lunged forward with his own claws. They raked across the ghast's chest, tearing through its flesh. The ghast let out a screech of pain and backed away.

Val took advantage of the ghast's momentary weakness and charged forward again. This time, he landed a blow that sent the creature reeling. It stumbled backward and fell to the ground, its eyes wide with fear. Val didn't hesitate. He pounced on the ghast and delivered a final killing blow, ripping its head completely off.

The creature's body went limp in his arms. Val stood up, panting heavily. He looked down at the crypt ghast's lifeless body and felt a sense of relief wash over him. But he knew that they weren't out of danger yet.

He whirled around to confront his friends, their faces twisted in panic. None had ever encountered a demon werewolf before, and the mere sight of it sent shivers of dread down their spines. The atmosphere was so charged with terror that they felt like they had been plunged into an abyss of fear.

Drak's voice was barely above a whisper as he grabbed Nephrym's arm and said, "Nephrym, talk to him. Make sure he knows who you are and that we're not a threat." He slowly turned his head towards the beast, now only a few yards away, his heart pounding in his chest.

Nephrym trembled as he looked upon Val, his emerald eyes wet with tears. He clasped his hands together in an imploring gesture and pleaded, "We are all safe now, Val, thanks to you. Our child and our friends are safe. Please, come back to me. Do not give in." He shuddered as he felt the darkness gripping Val's heart, crushing him from within. Only Nephrym had the power to free Val from this extraordinary peril and salvage him from the clutches of this demonic possession.

Val's usually gentle gaze had been replaced by a burning intensity. His pupils were an unnatural, deep crimson red and slit like the eyes of a goat. He stood stiffly in front of them, but his gaze was distant, as if he wasn't really there. Nephrym didn't seem to notice any change, but each member of the party exchanged glances and stepped back warily. They had all seen demon possessions and knew things had just gotten worse.

Grommellion spoke with conviction as he grasped Nephrym's hands. His touch was cold, but the warmth of his words comforted him. He had an air of anticipation about him as he stared deeply into her eyes.

"I would never hurt you," he said solemnly, tightening his grip. "You are the one who will bring our son to this world and give him life. I am Grommellion the Dark One, and soon our time will come."

Val had spiraled out of control, the reality of their fates crashing onto them with every passing second. Tales of ruin and destruction echoed through their minds as they remembered the stories Val had shared with Nephrym.

Entire villages were obliterated; not even a single child was left standing among mountains of ashes and corpses. A paralyzing fear filled their hearts as they wondered if Val would ever return from the depths of madness he'd descended into.

Grommellion towered over the group, his massive frame silhouetted against the setting sun. His voice echoed like thunder as he sneered down at them. "Why does Val deign to give you any value? You're nothing but a sorry collection of withered flesh and brittle bone!"

Val's trembling hands moved in erratic patterns, his eyes darting around the room frantically as he tried to find an escape from the force that held him captive. His body was contorted by the invisible grip, and the desperation on his face was clear.

The weight of their burden settled heavily upon each member of the group as they pondered how to free Val from the dark being that had taken over his mind.

Nephrym tenderly grasped Val's hand and placed it against his tear-streaked cheek. His voice, now a sorrowful hush, whispered, "Because they are my friends, your friends. We must make it out alive. I need them." He shuddered as he felt the darkness gripping Val's heart, crushing him from within. Only Nephrym had the power to free Val from this extraordinary peril and salvage him from the clutches of this demonic possession.

Val trembled, his arms shaking as he braced himself against the demon's onslaught. His only hope was to face it head-on and take back control. It had already claimed too much, and if he failed now, there would be nothing left of his life as he now knew it. He couldn't let that happen, no matter what the cost - so he clenched his teeth and pushed forward into that abyss of darkness with a strength he didn't know he possessed.

Lupine watched as Nephrym's face fell, the light in his eyes fading. He was taking Val's situation hard; it wasn't fair, not after all they'd gone through together. Lupine tried to lighten the mood with a joke, "Val... who's gonna be around to laugh at my gnome on a stick jokes if you're not here?" But even his attempt at humor couldn't break the heavy atmosphere.

Val felt an unfamiliar yet powerful energy surge through him. An authoritative voice boomed inside his head, more commanding than anything he had ever heard before.

"Your time is nearly at hand, Grommellion. Submit to your purpose." Intense pain seared through Val like a scorching blade slicing into his flesh. He dropped to his knees, clutching his head tightly as an agonizing scream tore from his lips.

Nephrym felt their unborn child writhing in joyful agony inside of him, sending a demonic message to Grommellion. A warning that it was too soon for him to take control. This unborn abomination, sharing flesh with its host, was far more malevolent and mercurial than Val could ever be - a wicked entity hell-bent on torture and destruction.

Grommellion's hands suddenly opened as he uttered a gut-wrenching apology in a whisper. His head hung low, weighed down by an invisible burden of guilt and regret. Val raised his eyes to the group, searching for understanding and forgiveness. Val was finally back in control. The air around them seemed to stand still, heavy with fear.

"What have I done? No. What DIDN'T I do? I'm such a fool." Val's mind raced, his eyes darting from one side of the room to the other as he searched for any sign of acceptance. They had all seen this momentary lapse of control - but would they ever forgive him? He stifled a sob and tried to find his voice as he peered upon them with tear-filled eyes. "I'm sorry, guys. Please, tell me you know that deep down, I'd never mean to hurt you…"

Nephrym lay on the cold stone floor, unable to speak or open his eyes. His body bucked and writhed, sending tremors of pain surging through him as fur began to sprout from every inch of exposed skin. His bones seemed to bend and contort beneath his flesh, reshaping him into a creature of the night. All the while, nobody noticed his transformation in the chaos caused by Val's possession.

Lupine's eyes widened in shock as he saw Nephrym lying in a heap on the cold, hard stone floor. His heart raced, and his mouth dropped open, a single phrase slipping out of his lips: "Holy shitballs!" He raced over to Nephrym's side, kneeling beside him and gently shaking his shoulder while screaming his name: "Nephrym! Are you ok?"

Nephrym roared and lashed out with his curled, clawed fingers, making contact with Lupine's chest and propelling him through the air. His back slammed against the wall with a thud before he hit the floor in a daze.

Val stepped forward, putting himself between Nephrym and the rest of the party.

"It's okay," he said calmly. His voice was a soothing balm meant to ease his fear and desperation. He had been there before, in his shoes, and knew exactly what he was going through—the horror, the pain. Val slowly motioned for everyone to stand back and give them space.

"We are all here for you. I am here for you."

Chapter 11
It's So Cute & Fluffy/Can We Keep It?

Nephrym had been forced to shift earlier than expected, and Val knew that his father was the only one with the power to make him do so. But how? It couldn't have been the full moon since it wasn't due for weeks yet.

Val felt a knot grow in his stomach as he tried to understand what could be causing such an unexpected shift for Nephrym. He had not yet undergone the rite of the pack. This should not be happening. There had to be something wrong. Terribly wrong.

Could it be the power of the lich's staff? Nephrym was not a true-born lycanthrope, nor had he completed the rite of the pack. He was not yet a werewolf. Then how?

Nephrym's fur bristled, his eyes wild, and a deep growl escaped as he bared his teeth. Barnabiz chuckled and shook his head. His imposing frame towered over Nephrym, not an ounce of fear in him. "You should all run...NOW!" Nephrym snarled, saliva dripping from his muzzle.

"Run from a little pup like you? I shit bigger after a large breakfast," Barnabiz harrumphed. "Better get your little pet before I have to clean its innards off of my maul."

Val's face contorted with anger as he stepped forward, fists clenched and teeth gritted. He pointed a quivering finger at the large ogre standing in front of him and shouted, "Touch him and you die, you big ogre fuck!" His voice echoed off the walls as he rose up to his full height. "Back off," he commanded, his voice steady now, "I told you all I have this under control."

Lupine clenched his fists as he glared at Val, who stood only steps away. His entire body quivered with rage. "Go ahead," he spat venomously, "Give me a reason why I shouldn't just gut you here and now for what you've done to my friend. He's done nothing to you, and look at him – he doesn't deserve this!"

Without warning, Nephrym lunged forward and plowed into Lupine like a charging bull. His momentum sent them both tumbling across the icy stone floor. Lupine let out a startled yelp as he felt his back slam against the hard ground. He couldn't believe what was happening--Nephrym, his long-time friend, was attacking him.

"Holy shit! Get off of me!" Lupine cries as Nephrym sinks his razor-sharp teeth into his neck. Scarlet liquid gushed from the wounds like a raging river, soaking both them and the surrounding floor. With one last shudder of pain, Lupine's eyes rolled back in his head, and he slumped to the ground, unconscious.

Nephrym slowly lifted his head, scanning the room with a demonic smirk. His eyes locked with each of his friends in turn, triggering a cacophony of memories. The sadness for what he had done welled up inside him, while at the same time, he felt a dark hunger stirring. He could almost feel himself moving to fulfill his destiny - an unstoppable force pushing to take their lives, as though he were only a spectator to his own actions.

Val's eyes were wide with fear and desperation as he grabbed hold of Nephrym's shoulders in a viselike grip. He was shaking, and his pleading voice contained a mix of sorrow and rage.

"Nephrym! You have to stay strong! Please, don't make me do this!" Val knew that unless Nephrym could get a handle on the situation, he would eventually be forced to join in the killing spree, doing something that would haunt him forever. Yet another dark memory haunts his nightmares as he tries to sleep each night.

A chill had entered the room, beginning at the top of one's scalp and shivering down their backs like a finger trailing in its wake. The low, echoing laughter had no discernible source yet seemed to reverberate from every corner of the room. And with it, an uneasy aura of evil seeped from the very walls.

A thin figure wearing a long, black hooded cloak leaning upon a large wooded staff carved into a wolve's head at the top stood in the center of the room. His voice, barely more than a whisper, echoed off the walls as he spoke. "Are we all ready to die now? Or shall we have some fun first?".

Val's face paled as he recognized the hooded figure before him. His gnarled hands clutched at his sword handle, and his heart raced. The Lich Lord Nivlac stood before them like a ghostly wraith of death, cold eyes peering out from beneath his cowl. "Leave us be or meet your maker, you worthless bag of bones," Val spat, steeling himself for what was to come.

Lich Lord Nivlac

Drak sank to his knees beside Lupine, whose face was pale and clammy. Drak carefully placed his hands over the jagged neck wound, feeling its warmth and the slickness of blood on his fingers.

Clenching his eyes shut, he whispered a quick prayer for healing, hoping it would be enough to keep Lupine alive until he could heal him properly.

Nephrym felt as if he'd been plunged into icy water. His gaze remained transfixed on the towering Lich, its arms outstretched and eyes ablaze with power. The werewolf trembled in fear, his small frame trembling underneath the Lich's control. He was like a puppet, and the lich was the puppeteer.

The Lich Lord's voice resonated through the chamber, echoing off the walls like thunder. His contorted face twisted into a mask of rage, and he unleashed a deafening scream that shattered the silence. "You are mine now!" he roared, pointing at us with his bony finger. "All of you! How dare you think that you can violate the sanctity of my tomb and live!" His words sent shivers down their spines, and they knew they were all in for a fight for our very lives.

Val's heart pounded as he snapped upright abruptly, his eyes wide with terror. He knew the lich's sinister plan was to take him, too. If the undead creature managed to control both werewolves, their fates would be sealed and there was no escape in sight. Val could feel the power of the lich's staff as its power raked over him, trying to grasp control.

Drak's face hardened as he looked at Auorak. "We have no other choice; you must do it. If we don't knock out Nephrym and Val, they'll be controlled by that thing." His voice trembled as he begged for the impossible. But it was the only real solution he could think of, and he knew, deep in his heart, that Auorak was the only one who could do it without truly harming them.

Auorak quickly raised both hands, his eyes wide as he faced Nephrym and Val. He leaned closer to them, and his gaze was like that if burning embers.

Auorak's lips pulled into a crooked grin, and he began to chant softly in the ancient language of magic. His voice rose and fell in tune with the words of his spell, his tone becoming more confident, more powerful as he surreptitiously inched one foot forward.

With a sharp intake of breath, he pointed at both Nephrym and Val at once and punched out the last syllables of his spell with extra gusto. Both of them fell limp and lifeless to the ground as the spell crashed into them like a wave.

The lich howled in fury as they pointed an accusing bony finger towards Auorak. With a shattering screech, it uttered the word "MORS!" and a sickening wave of green energy exploded forth from its finger, ripping through the air with a deafening roar. It crashed into Auorak with the force of a thousand lightning bolts, slamming him to the ground as his body writhed in pain.

Auorak lay on the cold stone floor, unable to move, the pain unbearable. His chest heaved, and spasms coursed through his limbs as he stared wide-eyed at the ceiling. Sweat beaded on his forehead despite the chill of the room. He knew that if it wasn't for the magical wards and protections he had in place, the spell would have successfully killed him.

Barnabiz's face twisted in rage as a deep guttural howl escaped his lips. His eyes flashed red in the dim light, and he charged toward the lich, singing an old ogre ballad of warriors marching off to their doom. The massive maul was raised high over his head, ready to be brought down with crushing force.

Drak's body trembled as he silently uttered a prayer to the gods. He raised his arm and clenched his fist, and a stream of flame gushed forth from his palm like a geyser, snaking its way through the air toward the lich. The bright pillar twisted and shimmered, filling Drak with an inner power from the gods themselves as it raced forward.

Drak's face was distorted with unbridled rage and hatred as he screamed at the top of his lungs. "Burn you son of a bitch! Climb back into the abyss that spawned you!" His voice thundered like thunder, vibrating with an intensity that could shake mountains.

The lich stood still and unyielding as Barnabiz's maul flew through the air in a vain attempt to strike it, while Drak's spell fizzled out just inches away. Its lips curled into a sinister smile, and its deep voice reverberated off the walls as it spoke: "So that is all you can do? How utterly disappointing."

Auorak gasped for air as he spoke, his voice strained and weak. "The bastard is phasing himself in and out of reality. That's why we can't seem to hit him with anything!" He braced himself against the wall, trying to take a few deep breaths. Trying to gather himself for one more spell.

Val's muscles tensed as he regained consciousness. Finding

himself collapsed on Nephrym, he wrapped his arms around the other werewolf's body. Nephrym snarled and growled as he started to wake. He struggled against Val's grip while a fierce battle of wills raged between him and the lich.

Nephrym felt Val's warm breath on his neck as Val whispered in his ear: "Use your strength to fight him. Do not give in." Val used his body as a shield to protect Nephrym from the horrific battle that was going on around them. His words body Nephrym's shield as he fought to expel the lich from his mind.

The lich's bony hands gripped the staff tightly as its skeletal grin widened. "You are of no use to me, none of you. I desire only the child." His ancient voice creaked with a strength greater than his form suggested, chanting in a forgotten language. "Infernus ab intus ardebit! Infernus vos consumet!" A glowing red light began to emerge from the tip of his staff, growing brighter and stronger by the second.

The stone floor below their feet seemed to seethe with energy, the dark grey slowly turning a deep, angry red. The heat intensified until it felt as if they all were standing in an oven, sweat dripping down their faces.

Auorak's throat felt dry as he opened his mouth to scream the incantation. He gestured wildly with his hands, sweat dripping down his face and stinging his eyes. "Gelu de mane tunica hanc terram!" His voice came out faint and raspy, yet still strong enough to fill the air around him.

A heavy fog of mist swirled around the room; the air was so cold it was almost stinging. The heat from a moment ago had been replaced by an icy chill. Everyone glanced nervously at each other as they felt the frost creeping up their arms and legs.

Barnabiz's face contorted in rage as his maul came crashing down, the force of the blow sending the lich flying backward. Sparks from its impact still crackled in the air as Barnabiz shouted, "What have you done? First, we were roasting alive and now this? Let's kill this bastard once and for all and be done with it already!"

Drak took a deep breath and lifted his arms to the sky. His voice thundered through the barren landscape as he called upon the gods for justice. "Audite me dii, ultione et furore ferite inimicos meos," he intoned with fervor, channeling all his rage into the words. The wind swirled around him, flinging sand and grit every which way.

A brilliant white light erupted from Drak, licking the air with its blinding intensity. He gritted his teeth and clenched his fists, channeling an immense surge of power that coalesced into a single beam of divine might that bombarded the lich. The force of the attack rippled through Drak's body, leaving him trembling as it tore through the creature. When the light faded away, the lich lay limp and lifeless on the ground.

Nephrym's face twisted in panic as he scrambled to extricate himself from Val's arms. He stumbled backward, and tears of relief welled up in his eyes when his friend didn't attempt to stop him. He rushed across the room, heedless of the danger that lurked there, and knelt beside his fallen comrade. His voice broke with emotion as he said, "I'm so sorry. I wanted to stop, but I couldn't control it."

Val stepped cautiously towards the motionless lich, his heart pounding in anticipation. He reached out and gingerly grasped the staff from its lifeless hand. A powerful energy surged through him, a warmth spreading through every inch of his body. His eyes widened as he realized he now held the power to make himself the true ruler of all lycanthropes in the Land of Dodd.

Lupine groaned as he sat up, his head spinning from the blood loss. His gaze fell upon his weeping friend, and he felt a swell of sorrow in his chest.

"I know it wasn't you," he said softly. "He paid for what he did. Now it's time to make him pay some more."

Lupine stood slowly and took in his surroundings. He spotted a small silver candlestick atop a shelf on the wall. He grasped it firmly in one hand and then made his way toward the lich. Taking a dagger from his boot, he sliced open the back of its robe with one deft motion. With the candlestick raised high above his head, Lupine lunged forward and thrust it into the lich's behind. "Anyone got a flint and steel?" he asked.

Auorak's laugh echoed through the chamber, reverberating off the walls. His finger trembled as he pointed it at the lich, and a guttural word rumbled from his throat. "Ustilo!" A brilliant flame arose from the lich's remains, engulfing it in an inferno of white-hot flames.

Drak exhaled deeply as he slid down the wall, grateful to have finally escaped the lich's grasp. He could feel his body beginning to relax, and the tightness in his chest began to fade.

"Let us mend our wounds and take a rest here," he said, his voice low and tired. "The lich will not be back anytime soon."

Blood Moon Rising

Lupine's face turned red as he yelled in disbelief. His fists clenched as he slammed them against the wall and shouted, "What do you mean he will not be back anytime soon? We just killed that bastard!" The room echoed with his anger.

Auorak roared out in agony, the excruciating pain of fractured ribs radiating through his chest with every breath. His hands trembled as he tried to stabilize the broken bones from the crushing force of the lich's magical attack. "It was a lich, you goblin dolt! We may have destroyed its corporeal form, but the only way to completely destroy it is to find and destroy its phylactery!"

Bryan Kurt Dodd

Chapter 12

To See The Moon Again

After a few fitful hours of sleep, the adventurers stirred from their makeshift beds. Their eyes were heavy, and they felt stiff from resting in the cold stone chamber of the lich's stronghold. They looked around, trying to shake off the remnants of slumber as they gathered their supplies for the daunting task ahead; Retnimle had sent them on a mission to find ancient artifacts hidden within the depths of this cursed place.

Drak narrowed his eyes as he examined the staff that Val was still gripping tightly in his hands. "I'm sure this is one of the artifacts we were sent to retrieve. But what else could this place be hiding?" He wondered out loud, turning slowly to scan the room.

Val's grip on the staff tightened so much that his knuckles turned white with strain. His face, menacing, he uttered the words through gritted teeth: "The staff is my birthright. Retsnimle works for my father and, therefore, works for me."

"Slow down there, wolf boy. I know you and Little Fluffy have not had any alone time to work on that pent-up frustration, but you need to chill." Lupine laughed as he rose to his feet. "Besides, who cares as long as we get paid."

Val's voice grew desperate, and her hands trembled as she spoke. "You do not understand. My father can not possess this staff. With it, he will have the power to control all the lycanthropes in the Land of Dodd — Nephrym and I included." He paused, searching Auorak's face for understanding.

"I thought the staff had no effect upon you, Val?" Auorak asked, his brow furrowing in confusion as he tried to make sense of what Val was saying.

Val's eyes flashed with an inner fire as he spoke. "My father is a demon-wolf like myself. We both have the ability to unlock the staff's full potential - powers that eluded even the lich. Powers my father cannot and will not possess." He raised his hands as if presenting the staff to the others. "In the hands of my father, he will make the eternal blood moon rise."

Lupine looked around at the dank, crumbling walls of the chamber they were in. He exhaled heavily as he tugged his tattered cape tighter around himself. "Let's give the staff and whatever else we find in this hell hole to Retsnimle and be done with this journey," he said, his voice weary and tired. "What is done with them after that is of no concern to us. I'm ready to go back to our normal lives."

Auorak strode towards the young lad, his heart pounding in his chest as he demanded, "What do you mean when you say your father will bring about the rise of the eternal blood moon?" His voice echoed through the darkened fields, resounding off every blade of grass, and he felt a chill run down his spine as the lad's cold eyes stared back at him.

"With the rising of the prophecied blood moon, the fate of all creatures of the night will be sealed. If the prophecy came true - a demon werewolf would rule over them with an iron claw, and the perpetual scarlet hue of the blood moon would saturate the sky and herald eternal darkness for the Land of Dodd." Drak trembled as he spoke of this ancient omen, his voice laced with despair and terror. "A dread will rise from the darkest depths of the abyss, a harbinger of destruction and death. It is said that it will bring about the demise of the Lord of Light himself, an end of days for all who serve the Lord of Light in the Land of Dodd."

Nephrym's voice trembled with emotion as he spoke, tears streaming down his face. "The staff goes nowhere. Whoever has that staff will own me, Val, and you, Lupine. Why do you think the lich made me attack you? You're one of us now. And I refuse to hand my free will over to an evil dictator." His knuckles whitened as he wrenched the staff from Val and clenched it tightly, feeling the weight of it in his hands and the finality of the words he had just spoken. He took a deep breath before collapsing to his knees on the chill stone floor, overwhelmed by a wave of guilt for what felt like handing his friend a death sentence.

Lupine's shouts echoed through the room as his face twisted in anger and disbelief. "What do you mean I'm one of you?! I won't be a part of your sick, demented werewolf cult!" His voice was laced with venom as he spat out his words like acid. "How could you do this to me? You were a brother to me."

Nephrym's voice trembled and cracked as he spoke, tears streaming down his face. His fists were clenched so tightly around the staff that his knuckles turned a pale white. He looked at each of them with a profound sense of sorrow, regret, and desperation. "I could not stop myself from doing it, I swear. I would have taken my own life before I harmed any of you. Let alone sentence you to a life unwillingly bound to the moon."

Val's eyes filled with compassion as he watched Nephrym struggle with his newfound identity. He reached out and touched his shoulder, trying to put her friend at ease. "Look Lupine, there are a lot of awesome things that come along with being a lycanthrope," he said.

Auorak's heart raced as he frantically stuffed his belongings into a sack, the imminence of danger looming like a rabid dog. "We have to get outta here - now! That lich will come back, and it'll be beyond livid after having a candlestick jammed up its ass and then set on fire!" He shuddered at the thought of the wrath that awaited them if they failed to escape this place swiftly. "We will not be so lucky a second time."

Barnabiz scratched his chin, examined the staff in Nephrym's hands, and asked in a worried tone, "We are still one magical thingy short, aren't we?"

With a shudder of revulsion, Drak barked out an order. "It has to be here! Lupine and Nephrym - search the lich's corpse for anything we might have missed!" His stomach churned as they rummaged through the stinking body, desperate to uncover an overlooked clue in the remains of their enemy.

Barnabiz's face twisted in disgust, and he clapped a hand over his nose and mouth as a thick wave of putrid stench assaulted him. "Holy hells," he managed to say through gritted teeth, "that is a stench worthy of a plague." His eyes watered as he surveyed the rotting corpse lying before them. "Whatever magics were keeping that thing's body intact have obviously worn off," he observed. He turned to his companion with a rueful smile. "Remember to cut out the femur bones for me. We will eat like kings next; we camp under the sky."

Val's face contorted with disgust as he kneels protectively beside a shuddering Nephrym. "No way in the hell would we consume anything you prepared!" He exclaims in revulsion, voice dripping with acid. "You expect us to eat food cooked with parts of that damned lich? You must be truly twisted and depraved." Val spat out, fists clenching and unclenching at his sides.

Barnabiz's eyes glowed with a sinister intensity as he let loose an evil, guttural laugh that echoed through the night air. "You have no clue of the depths of depravity to which I can sink, lad," he hissed maliciously. "I do not abide by morality or laws; all that matters is survival. The atrocities I've committed in the pursuit of survival will haunt your nightmares for eternity. Besides, don't knock it until you try it. Lich bone stew is quite the treat."

Lupine stumbled out from behind the lich's corpse, holding a long, slim wand. His face was pale, and his eyes were watery, and a rancid stench clung to him like a garment. "We found a wand of staff, that's it," he choked out. "You gotta spell this stench away. I think I'm going to pass out!"

Drak's eyes were wide and eager; his face lit up with excitement. "Good, let's get the hell out of here," he said as he stepped towards the door. He took a deep breath and longed for the feeling of being outside, to feel the warmth of the sun on his skin and see the stars twinkling in the night sky.

Nephrym felt something new - an unfamiliar yet comforting presence. He sensed an energy in the air that seemed to fill him up and ease his inner turmoil as if a long-lost part of himself had been found. He closed his eyes to better absorb the soothing vibes and faintly heard voices of joy emanating from deep within him. The staff was calling out to him and his unborn child.

Nephrym's adrenaline surged as he instinctively gripped the staff as if it had been his for years. He realized that if it fell into Val's father's hands, it would be a death sentence for all lycanthropes in the

Land of Dodd, and he had to find a way to secure it before it was too late. With every fiber of his being focused on retaining the staff, Nephrym knew that this was the only chance for him - and everyone else - and failure was not an option.

Auorak ripped the wand from Lupine's hands with a violent tug. "We've got the item we were paid for. We need to get out of this death trap before it can take us down!" His voice was charged with urgency as he raced towards the exit, not daring to look back. They needed to escape now or never.

Bryan Kurt Dodd

Chapter 13
I Saw The Light/OMG, It's Bright

The party struggled onward as they plodded through the vast elven ruins with a sense of dread escalating in their minds. For two days, they trudged on, finding respite only when absolute exhaustion stopped them in their tracks. With the lich gone -- for now at least -- its malevolent traps and enchantments no longer posed a threat, but the feeling of impending doom lingered like a sickly fog in the air.

The adventurers trudged up the never-ending stairwell, each step a stepping stone of hope after an eternity of darkness. Each of them was filled with a frenzied anticipation to emerge from the depths and once again feel the sun's warmth on their faces, to behold the sun shining bright in the midday sky. Every step closer brought greater joy but also fear - for what lies ahead of them.

As they emerged from the tunnel, the glare of the sun nearly blinded Val. He squinted and saw looming figures on horseback at the entrance to the surface. A cacophony of clanging armor and whinnying horses filled his ears.

The vibrations of their footsteps shook the very ground beneath his feet, threatening to throw him off balance. It wasn't just one or two soldiers, but hundreds of them—a full encampment with tents and watch-fires blazing in every direction.

Val's father stood before them, a tall figure illuminated by the bright sun behind him. His piercing gray eyes studied Val and his friends before settling on him. "Welcome back, my son," he said with a gentle yet villainous smile. "It pleases me to see that you are well. Were you and your friends able to procure the items?"

Nephrym's face was wracked with rage as he snarled at Val's father. "We did not put our lives on the line for you!" he shouted, his spit flying through the air. "These artifacts are ours and ours alone! We will see them to Retsnimle and no one else!" His voice echoed, reverberating with a sense of finality.

Barnabiz's voice boomed like thunder across the battlefield. "You heard the pipsqueak! Now, turn and be on your way or suffer the consequences!" he bellowed with an icy fury that chilled even the most seasoned of Val's father's warriors. "Remove yourself from our path and bugger off!"

"I am the one in charge here! Retsnimle works for me, which means that all of you work for me was well. Best you learn your place and heed your king's warning lest you anger him. Hand over the staff and wand this instant, or else my royal guards will take it from your cold, lifeless hands. Don't test me, Val - I won't warn you again."

Nephrym could feel the staff's ancient energy surging through him, pulsing in urgent demand. He heard a ghostly whisper reverberate through his mind: "Say the word, my master, and I shall take control of them all. They will fall to their knees and bow before you and the righteous power you alone command. Your reign shall extend over the entire Land of Dodd." The staff's tempting words filled Nephrym with a burning desire for power.

Val's father leaped from his horse with a thunderous rumble as both feet hit the ground and stormed up to Val, his scowl burning through the air like a searing maelstrom. His gauntlet-clad hand lashed out at him in an instant, smacking him across the face with such force it left him reeling. "Do not disobey me!" he roared. "You will do as I commanded - kill them all now! Do it now, Val!" His voice echoed like thunder off the surrounding hillsides.

Drak stepped in between Val and his father, roaring with fury. "I'm warning you, Lord, whatever your name is! It's time for you and your men to get out of here right now!" His voice rumbled like a storm and left no room for negotiation. "You are no king we serve."

Nephrym raised the staff above his head, gripping it so tightly that his knuckles turned white. Fury burned in his eyes as he stared down Val's father and the hundreds of guards that stood before him. "Leave now or suffer the consequences! I will show no mercy, and you have no right to any of this! Val is mine! He and my friends are under my protection - go now while you still can, or face a wrath like nothing you've ever seen!"

Rage seethed in Val's father's voice as he spoke, "Silly pup. You will learn your place just as my son will learn his. Dare not to think you can meddle in affairs which your feeble mind cannot comprehend." His hand shot out suddenly, clasping the pommel of his sword.

"Take them, take them all!" Nephrym screamed out. Speaking to the staff as he pleaded for it to aid him and his friends. "I command you to make every lycanthrope before I bend a knee to me!"

A blinding light exploded from the staff, radiating a powerful energy that sent every lycanthrope but Nephrym to the ground in surrender. The staff pulsed with power, whispering voluptuously back at him, "Your enemies tremble before you, my liege. Command them now."

Nephrym's voice boomed with authority as he now commanded not only the lycanthropes before him but all the lycanthropes of the Land of Dodd. His eyes burned white, and his words seared into their minds.

"Rip every limb, every tooth and every nail from Lord Vladimir Val'Rak's body. Leave only his eyes for the crows to peck from his rotting corpse." The intensity of Nephrym's gaze seemed to freeze them in place. "Let him find what true suffering is."

Their steps were heavy and determined as they marched in unison towards Lord Vladimir Val'Rak. Steel glinted in the sunlight as weapons were drawn, accompanied by guttural growls of anticipation. The legion moved with practiced ease, each slash of a blade or swing of an axe as precise and deadly as the last. In what seemed like brief moments, the once proud and benevolent lord lay prone on the battlefield, surrounded by his former subjects and bathed in his own blood.

Nephrym trudged through the blood to Lord Vladimir Val'Rak's body. His hands shook as he carefully reached for the crown that sat atop the corpse's now bloodied and misshapen skull. He stood, rubbing his thumb along the edge of the gold circle before turning to face young Val. He walked with reverence and kneeled before him, raising the crown up in respect and offering it to him.

Nephrym knelt before Val, holding the golden crown in his hands. It was encrusted with rubies and sapphires, glinting in the light of the full moon.

"You are now the King of Gastovia," said Nephrym solemnly. "King of all the lycanthropes in the Land of Dodd. Take it and claim your birthright." Val felt a surge of emotion surge through him as he reached out and accepted the crown. "This is my gift to you, my lord Val."

An electric current ran through Val as he gingerly placed the crown on his head. His eyes widened as a noisy rumble filled the air, and wisps of magic swirled around him.

A flood of memories washed over him; though unfamiliar, he instinctively knew they belonged to the previous rulers of the land. With this knowledge, Val felt power, unlike any other surge through his veins.

Val stumbled back, shock registering on his face. He watched as Nephrym dropped to the ground like a stone thrown in a pond. His skin was ghostly pale, and his cheek felt cold when Val reached down to touch it. A deep sorrow settled in Val's heart as he realized that the last person who truly mattered to him was slowly dying. The beginning of the end had begun.

The guards quickly obeyed the command, picking up the limp body of the small gnome. His clothes hung off him now, revealing an emaciated frame and cuts and bruises that covered his skin. He was slowly being killed from the inside as his very soul and life force were feeding the demonic entity inside of him. The guards rushed to keep pace with their leader as he shouted orders at a hurried pace. "If he dies, consider your lives forfeit." Fear was visible in every one of their faces.

Val quickly climbed atop his father's horse, its powerful muscles rippling beneath him. He cast a glance back to the rest of the group, determination flashing in his eyes. "My friends, I must go," he said. "Gather your courage and your weapons and follow me to Gastovia; we will make ready for your arrival."

Val spurred his horse forward, and the animal surged ahead, hooves pounding against the hard ground. The entire legion quickly dispersed as Val and his horse rapidly left the others behind, their figures shrinking to a tiny dot on the horizon as they gained distance with every bounding stride.

Lupine's face was drained of color, and his hands were shaking as he looked around the square. "What the fuck just happened here?" he muttered. He stepped closer to the figure on the ground, eyes wide in disbelief. "Did we just watch an assassination? Did Nephrym just kill the king of Gastovia and make his boyfriend the new king?"

The large ogre shook with laughter, deep and booming. His mouth was fixed in a wide grin, and his eyes twinkled mischievously as he boomed: "Aye, and I think your wee friend just became the queen!"

Drak's eyes widened as he surveyed the group and the activity that took place before him. He shook his head in disbelief. "I am not so sure that there is any of our friends left in there," Drak remarked solemnly.

"The Nephrym we all knew would never condone such an act and most certainly would not be the one carrying it out. I have stared into the eyes of evil before and saw them look back. I saw the same as Nephrym looked upon us."

Lupine clenched his fists and shut his eyes tight, fighting back tears. His voice shook with emotion as he spoke. "No matter! We do whatever we have to do; we can't just sit here while Nephrym is out there somewhere. He's like a brother to me. To all of us."

Auorak's voice was filled with determination as he spoke. "Then to Gastovia, we go. Besides, I cannot help but feel that our young Val has left us with an unfinished mission and needs our help." He declared. "And we have not yet been paid."

Barnabiz snorted, his face twisted in indignation. "The only help that young pup is in need of is to help his head find its way upon a pike," he growled, jabbing an angry finger at the air. "There will be blood soon. The blood moon calls for it. May as well be his and those that have wronged us."

Chapter 14

Are We There Yet?

The group stood in stunned silence, unable to process what had just happened. After a few moments of silence, their minds cleared, and the only thing they could agree upon was that they must travel to Gastovia and save Nephrym, no matter the cost. Each person steeled themselves for the journey ahead, knowing that their fate hung upon it.

Barnabiz sighed and put his hand on Nephrym's shoulder, watching the tears well up in his eyes. "I'm sorry, little goblin," he began softly. "The elves and demons played this game, and the demons always win. Always. And as much as I hate elves, I hate demons even more. The demon has taken him, transformed him into one of their own kind - a demon wolf. It is our duty to help him reach the gods, for they yearn for them because they are spurned by them and will never know that grace. And it is our duty to speed them on their way to meet them." He spoke slowly and deliberately, trying to make sure that Nephrym understood.

The figure of the ogre, looming above them and surrounded by the carnage that lay before them, was not one to be taken lightly. Everyone had looked into Barnabiz's deep black and soulless eyes, so full of loathing, and knew that his words were true.

As they trudged into the damp forest towards their destiny in Gastovia, all of them pondered if they could bring themselves to kill Nephrym when the time came if needed. Deep down, they all knew that was what awaited them, whether they were willing to accept it or not.

Auorak ran a hand through his hair, searching for courage as he spoke in a grave tone. "You all realize that we are about to face the lycanthrope nation in its entirety. We cannot just simply stroll right into Gastovia and kill off its new king and whatever Nephrym is there now. It will be our heads that sit atop the pikes at the castle gate." He glanced around at his comrades, their faces etched with worry at the thought of marching to imminent doom.

Drak grinned, and his eyes sparkled. "I know someone who will help us," he said, "and they're crazy enough to join us on this wild death ride."

Auorak walked among the small group of brave souls; his voice filled with awe and trepidation. "We're marching into a certain death," he said, shaking his head in wonder. "Who would be crazy enough to join us?"

"It is that damned fairy?" Barnabiz shouted in a thundering rage, the force of his voice ringing through the air. His eyes burned red with fury, and his fists clenched tightly as if he were preparing for battle against an unseen enemy. The ogre's voice was raspy, worn with worry. "That little bastard is crazy. He will kill us all or, at best, speed us on our way to the gods. He would sell his mother's soul for a copper coin!"

Drak's eyes were like chips of ice as he spoke. His voice was measured and cold as he said, "Crazy is what we need. Someone who has the skills to get the job done yet lacks any moral compass in regard to how it is done." The other occupants of the room exchanged uneasy glances before shifting their gaze back to Drak.

Lupine clenched his fists, and his voice held a hint of desperation as he addressed the group. "We'll do whatever it takes to bring Nephrym back. No questions asked."

The group trudged down the dirt path, cloaked in an oppressive stillness. All that could be heard was the crunch of their footsteps and the occasional call of a crow from above. Dappled sunlight filtered through a canopy of oak trees as they ventured towards Gastovia - a destination that promised much but equally threatened danger. Could this be the final judgment for these four adventurers or simply a meeting between old friends?

Drak adjusted the strap of his satchel and stood with his arms crossed, looking intently at Auorak.

"Look," he said in a low voice, "Send a message to Fuckstockings. Have him meet us in the mountains just outside the valley entrance to Gastovia. And tell the little scoundrel to lay low until we give him more instructions." Drak paused for a moment as he mentally composed his next move, then added, "And make sure no one else is aware of our plans. Not that we actually have one yet."

Auorak closed his eyes and whispered an ancient incantation, the very same one used to summon all sorts of foul creatures. His words echoed off the trees like a warning bell as he called upon Fuckstockings, the devious fairy assassin. They all knew that in order to survive what was ahead, each of them would soon have to make a sacrifice that may very well be their lives. None of them dared speak it out loud, but they all felt a chill of dread run down their spines.

Barnabiz scowled as he declared his dark promise, his eyes burning with unbridled fury. He curled his hands into tight fists and spat out each word with vehemence. "If that little winged rat betrays us," he seethed, "I will take pleasure as I rip his wings from his tiny corpse and eat them."

The ragtag group traveled onward toward Gastovia in hopes of rescuing their dear friend and comrade. An uneasy fear settled over the group as they trod through the darkening woods, a thick fog rolling in upon them, but they continued on, spurred by friendship and hope.

"The fog is thick as a wolf's pelt, so dense it could cloak the approach of those foul beasts until they're upon us. Look there," Barnabiz pointed to the sky, his finger shaking with dread. "The blood moon shines on adjoining nights -- an omen of death! We must be prepared ourselves for what is to come." His voice grew hoarse with each word, spitting out sharp sounds that hung like icicles in the night air.

"Relax, old friend. There will be no wolves at our door tonight. Nephrym will make sure of that. He may be in bed with the enemy, but he is still our friend." Auorak remarked, trying to calm the large ogre down. "There has to be something left of the gnome we all know."

Barnabiz's jaw clenched as he spat his words venomously, "The wolves are nothing compared to what one single demon can do. A single demon is a thousand times more deadly than an army of them." His gaze turned to the ground, not out of fear but with an intensity that promised all who heard it death if they disturbed him. "Death, I do not fear. Are you lot ready to die? Or would you rather be slaves to a demon?"

An unnatural stillness descended upon the group. Even the sounds of the night had ceased, and their voices seemed to echo in the thick air. A chill crept up their spines as apprehension filled the clearing. Someone – or something – was out there, lurking in the shadows. But what?

The unnatural fog grew ever denser the farther along their journey. The silence unnerved even the most courageous of the weary adventurers. Feelings of being watched grating upon them all. Yet not a single one of them knew where. It was like a giant broody shadow, and it grew thicker and heavier with every step they took. It was as if the trees themselves were voyeurs. The massive crimson moon tinted the fog an eerie blood red.

Lupine nervously glanced between Barnabiz and Drak as he matched their quick strides, barely keeping up. He spoke to the group, worry edging his voice. "My goblin sense is telling me something is wrong here - not our usual mischief. This time, I agree with Barnabiz."

Out of nowhere came the deep, baritone howls. The wolves were hunting, and their cries echoed through the forest. From every direction at once, they seemed to be coming. The pack was on the move, and everyone knew who their prey was.

Lupine's gut twisted, and his throat constricted as if a live wire were coiling inside of him. He fell to his knees in the middle of the road, writhing beneath the weight of that inexplicable agony. Through bleary eyes, he saw a spectral figure hovering over him - Nephrym. "Fear not," Nephrym said, his voice like a bell tolling in the stillness of the forest. "The wolves will accompany you to Gastovia." And then everything went black.

Auorak's fearful voice echoed off the walls as he shouted, "Do not touch him! Back away slowly. It could be a curse or enchantment; who knows what it can do?" He watched warily as his friends distanced themselves from the goblin lying motionless on the ground.

The goblin's body jerked and spasmed as air rushed back into his lungs, hardening in a sudden gasp of life. His eyes flew open wide with terror, and he trembled uncontrollably. He had looked into the eyes of death and felt its cold embrace.

The goblin forced himself to rise, every limb trembling with uncertainty. The harsh truth pulsed through him like icy daggers, threatening to tear apart his very being. He had to accept it; they could not save Nephrym, and the guilt of that knowledge manifested itself in a single salty bead that welled up from his eye and coursed down his sunbaked leathery green skin.

Trembling, the small goblin's gaze lowered to the dirt. His mind raced with fear and terror as if he'd just seen a ghost. "I saw him," he stammered, voice shaking. "He said the wolves were going to protect and guide us to Gastovia, but it wasn't him. Something was off. We may be safe for now. Maybe. If Val and Nephrym do not want us dead, what do we need protection from?"

The air was thick with a palpable tension as Drak surveyed the group and spoke. "We have two choices: go now and hope to survive to fight another day, or refuse and face a legion of werewolves. I choose survival," he proclaimed boldly, desperation flashing in his eyes.

A beat of silence hung over everyone before they reluctantly agreed to the only way they could remain alive. "And in the meantime, perhaps we can come up with a plan or pray that the gods are not done with us just yet."

Barnabiz's lips quivered as conflicting emotions surged through his veins. An urge to fight and an inclination to simply flee in equal measure warred within him, yet he steeled himself and pressed forth. "Aye, the moon is calling for blood," he said grimly. His eyes darted around fearfully, but determination glimmered in them. "By the Lord of Light, let's pray it is not ours it hungers for. We may be marked for death and our time short, but I say we drive the dagger as deep as we can in their wretched hearts as we breathe our last breath."

A chill ran through Auorak as the ogre's words reverberated in his mind. All his hopes for a peaceful resolution had been dashed; they'd be forced to confront the threat no matter what direction they took. He quaked with fear, taking a deep breath before he reluctantly conceded to the inevitable battle ahead. "The ogre speaks true. There is no turning from this fight. It will follow us wherever we go. Best we meet it head-on and be done with it." Auorak reluctantly agreed.

Barnabiz's lip curled into a sneer as he clenched his fists, his knuckles turning white. "So long as I get to rip the wings from that little fae bastard when we are done," he growled under his breath.

Drak's hand trembled as he reached for the goblin; his own nerves shot from the chaos they had just escaped. He could feel the weight of their decision settling heavily on his shoulders.

"We have no choice but to go to Gastovia and try to rescue Nephrym," he said through gritted teeth, trying to mask his fear. They were risking everything for their friend, and there was a good chance they wouldn't make it out alive. But Drak knew they couldn't live with themselves if they didn't try.

Whispers of ancient tales swirled in the air, speaking of demons, elves, and wolves locked in an eternal struggle for power. The desolate ruins of the elven kingdom loomed in the distance, a haunting reminder of their downfall. Barnabiz's heart raced with fear and anticipation as he prepared for the inevitable battle between the demonic forces and the howling wolves, both vying for control over the cursed Land of Dodd. Trapped in the midst of this nightmare, Barnabiz could only pray that he and his friends would make it out alive.

The weary party continued their journey towards Gastovia, each step feeling heavier than the last.

The thought of their friend being imprisoned and controlled by a demon weighed heavily on their hearts. And the possibility of him becoming a werewolf permanently like Val added to their fears. They all had an endless stream of questions, each more urgent than the last, desperately seeking answers to understand where they fit in this unfolding tale and what role they played in rescuing their friend.

Each mile felt longer than the last as they pushed forward with determination, driven by their love for their friend and the need to save him from whatever dark forces were at work.

"I do not like being flanked and watched by these mongrels! It is like they are hunting us." Drak smirked as he looked over to Barnabiz.

Auorak's voice trembled as he leaned in close, his eyes darting around fearfully. "We can't trust them," he hissed. "They're hunting us, waiting for the perfect moment to strike. We'll be helpless like lambs led to the slaughter." His words sent a chill down everyone's spine, making them realize the gravity of the situation. Our enemies are ruthless and cunning, and we were nothing but pawns in their twisted game.

Lupine's heart raced as he spoke to the group. "When we reach Gastovia, I will be the one who ends Nephrym's tortured existence if he cannot be saved," he confessed, his voice trembling with trepidation at the thought of condemning his closest friend to such a fate. Yet deep down, a twisted part of him desired to carry out this final, desperate act.

As the days stretched on, the forest grew thicker and darker, suffocating our journey towards Gastovia. Every step we took was accompanied by a sense of dread as if the wolves were lurking just beyond the shadows. We could feel their eyes upon us, waiting for the perfect moment to strike and unleash their savage fury should the order be given. None of us dared to speak of them, but their presence was suffocating, an ever-present threat that loomed over our every move.

Drak's eyes darted around, searching for any signs of danger. He leaned in close to Auorak, his voice trembling with fear and urgency. "We have to get a message to Fuckstockings," he breathed. "The wolves... they're watching us, aren't they? One wrong move, and we're dead. We need not give them a reason to make us their foe until we must."

Auorak leaned in close and whispered, "They'll sense the magic if I try to contact him. We need to be careful." He glanced over his shoulder, paranoid that someone might be listening.

As the sun began to dip below the horizon, the group of travelers set up their tents and started a fire. They knew it would be their final night in the wilderness before reaching Gastovia, so they savored their last moments of solitude under the starry sky and the blood-red moon.

The party huddled together around the flickering fire, their eyes darting nervously to the dark woods surrounding them. The wolves' howls seemed to echo endlessly, a haunting symphony that sent shivers down their spines.

Silent tension hung heavy in the air between the ogre, the dragonborn, and the goblin. Each one was keenly aware of the dangers ahead and the slim chances of survival for all three. Their fears and doubts weighed on them like a heavy fog, obscuring any hope for victory against the formidable enemy that awaited them in Gastovia.

Bryan Kurt Dodd

Chapter 15
Long Live The King

Val's body trembled as he knelt over Nephrym, his hands drenched in blood and gore. He could feel Nephrym's weak pulse flickering under his fingertips, barely clinging to life. His labored breaths were almost imperceptible, each one a desperate struggle to survive. He simply had to make it. He just had to.

The midwife's hands trembled as she held the squirming bundle in her arms. The piercing cry of the newborn filled the room, almost drowning out Nephrym's agonized screams. Blood and viscera coated the floor, remnants of what used to be his stomach and torso.

Despite his supernatural abilities, it was clear that survival was a long shot for Nephrym. No amount of lycanthrope healing could fix this gruesome damage. Death seemed inevitable, leaving the room cloaked in a thick aura of horror and darkness.

Val stood tall and proud, his chest puffed out as he declared, "He shall be called Nevrin of the House of Val, and he will be the greatest ruler to ever grace the Land of Dodd. And he shall rule it in its entirety." He plastered a smile on his face, pretending to be overjoyed by the birth of their son. But deep down, the thought of losing Nephrym tore at his heart, and he couldn't hold back the tears that welled up in his eyes. The weight of his sorrow was suffocating him, threatening to consume him whole.

Nephrym's body convulses as the unnatural fusion of lycanthrope and demonic energies courses through his veins. His bones snap and twist, muscles bulging and writhing as his body undergoes a violent transformation. Organs that were once torn and mutilated regenerate at an alarming rate, flesh knitting back together in a gruesome display of supernatural healing. The once-open wounds are now sealing shut, leaving behind only faint scars as Nephrym's body becomes something otherworldly.

With trembling hands, Val frantically checked Nephrym's pulse and could feel a faint flicker of life. Tears streamed down his face as Val let out a guttural cry of relief as he watched Nephrym's chest rise and fall with each labored breath. In that moment, Val felt an overwhelming surge of gratitude for everything the Land of Dodd had given him - his beloved son and his dear friend who had miraculously survived against all odds.

Nephrym's eyes snapped open, but they were no longer the bright, lively eyes of before. They were haunted, empty, as if they had glimpsed into the abyss and brought back a piece of it with them. His body felt heavy and cold as if death still lingered in his veins. He remembered the searing pain, the darkness that threatened to take him forever. And now, as he struggled to sit up, he could feel a presence looming over him, a price that must be paid for his return to the world of the living.

Val's eyes brimmed with tears as he gazed at Nephrym, relieved that he had survived the brutal birth. He nodded towards the midwife, who gently held up their newborn son in her arms. "Our son," Val whispered proudly. "His name shall be Nevrin, first of his name and heir to the House of Val. May he one day rule over our land with strength and compassion." Nephrym smiled through the exhaustion and leaned in to kiss Val, grateful for their son and hopeful for the future of their family.

"He shall indeed rule the Land of Dodd. But the Land of Dodd needs not a compassionate king. It needs a king that is willing to do whatever it takes to rule his people and maintain peace by whatever means necessary." Nephrym explained to Val.

Val shuddered as Nephrym's words echoed in his mind. The throne of Dodd was not one for a person of kindness or mercy. It was a seat that required ruthless determination and a willingness to do whatever it took to bridal its power and lead the people. Val couldn't help but feel a cold chill run down his spine as he now realized the true nature of the kingdom they served. It ruled them as much as they ruled it.

"And our son shall be that king." Val proclaimed to Nephrym and to the Land of Dodd.

With a commanding voice and regal air, King Val'Rak of House Val issues a proclamation that shall echo through the kingdom. The news shall be announced with great fanfare, trumpets will sound, and banners unfurl to celebrate the birth of High Prince Nevril, who is now heir to the throne of Dodd.

Val turns to a nearby servant and declares, "This sayeth I, King Val'Rak of House Val." His words carry weight and authority as they ring out across the land, marking this momentous occasion in the history of their noble kingdom.

On this day, in the Land of Dodd, a young baby was born. His arrival was marked by a convergence of bloodlines - that of angels, demons, and lycanthropes - all coursing through his tiny veins.

The very air tingled with anticipation as this harbinger of death made his entrance into the world. His mere presence seemed to stir up the elements, sending a shiver down the spines of all those who bore witness to his birth in this sacred land.

Chapter 16

Honey, I'm Home

The first hints of dawn peeked through the thick foliage, casting long shadows on the forest floor. Suddenly, a loud and unfamiliar sound pierced the peaceful morning - it was the blaring of distant trumpets. The campers stirred from their sleep, unsure of what was causing the commotion.

"From the sounds of it, our wee lil friend and his puppy are having a celebration," Barnabiz remarked as he himself wondered exactly what the occasion could be.

Lupine's face lit up with excitement as he announced, "Nephrym is safe! I just know it. We have to act fast and save him!" His words were filled with urgency and concern as he frantically paced the room, his mind racing with worry for his friend's well-being.

Auorak's eyes widened in fear, and he grabbed Drak's arm tightly. "It's happening," he whispered, his voice trembling. "Our darkest fear has come to pass. The child has been born." They both knew what that meant - the beginning of the darkness that would consume them all. A darkness that would blanket the entire Land of Dodd. Their worst fears were becoming reality before their very eyes.

Drak's eyes flickered with fear as he uttered a desperate prayer to the unknown forces that may have kept Nephrym alive through whatever hell he had faced. His voice trembled as he said a silent prayer to the Lord of Light for protection against this monstrous abomination that he knew they now would face, fearfully bowing his head.

Barnabiz grumbled as he loaded his weapons into a worn leather pack. "I swear those wolves never stop their infernal howling," he said to his companions. "Let's go take care of whatever needs killing today."

Lupine threw his head back with a hearty laugh as he packed up his belongings. "Come on, no secret ogre family recipes for wolf?" he joked, nudging Barnabiz with his elbow. Despite the dire situation at hand, Barnabiz couldn't help but crack a smile at his ridiculous antics.

"Might as well get this over with. Who knows, perhaps Val and Nephrym will be waiting for us. All of us being greeted with a hero's welcome for saving the queen." Auorak remarked, trying to continue the lightheartedness while it was still possible.

Lupine furrowed his brow and glanced between Auorak and Drak. "I must have taken quite a few more blows to the head than I recall," he muttered, "because I don't remember saving a queen." His puzzled expression spoke volumes about his confusion. "I think that I would remember a queen."

"Nephrym is the bloody queen, you nitwit." Barnabiz chuckled.

Lupine furrowed his brow, confusion evident in his voice. "Hold on, did I hear that right? Is Nephrym the queen? But he's not even a woman," he said, struggling to make sense of the situation.

Auorak struggled to explain the awkward situation to his friend. "You see, Val was recently crowned king after his father's death, and now he's... well, having relations with Nephrym, and I think they are a couple or something. So technically, Nephrym is the queen." Auorak cringed at the bizarre explanation, unsure of how else to describe the dynamic between the two friends.

"Oh...I get it now! Nephrym is Val's bitch. So, Nephrym is now the bitch queen. That is the proper name for a dog of that stature and title, is it not?" Lupine replied.

Drak's lips curled into a sly grin, and he let out a low chuckle. "Ah, something along those lines," he said, leaning in closer. "But let's keep it between us." His eyes twinkled mischievously as they all shared a humorous moment.

A sharp, explosive noise cut through the air, causing Barnabiz and his companions to jump. Suddenly, a small figure appeared between them, dressed in black, studded leather from head to toe. The figure smirked and addressed Barnabiz with a flirty tone, blowing a kiss towards him. "Did you miss me, tootles?"

With a swift swing of his massive maul, Barnabiz brought it down with a thunderous crash next to the tiny creature. It let out a shrill shriek and taunted, "You missed me, bitch!"

As the small figure brushed the dirt from its armor, his red and gold wings shimmering in the sunlight, everyone in the group braced themselves. They knew that with Fuckstocking's unpredictable nature, things could either go extremely well or disastrously wrong.

Drak clasped his hands together and bowed slightly. "We are eternally grateful for your arrival during this dire situation. I pray that our message reaches you in good health." He said with a tone of relief and gratitude. "I see you and the ogre have not lost that spark of love between you."

The fairy cackled, "He may act tough, but I know he's just a softy for me deep down. Like a grumpy cat with a heart of gold."

The ogre's voice rumbled like a hungry belly, and his beady eyes followed the small, winged creature with greed. "You must have nine lives like a cat, you pesky little pest," he snarled. "How in the world are you still alive?"

"Enough, both of you!" Auorak's voice rang out, cutting through the tense atmosphere.

"We have more pressing affairs to attend to than your petty lovers' quarrel. We must make haste for Gastovia Castle. The child has arrived, and I fear it could spell trouble for Nephrym as well as the entire land of Dodd." His brow furrowed as he spoke, his eyes darting between the two figures standing before him.

The urgency in his tone was palpable, and there was a sense of foreboding hanging heavy in the air. This was no time for bickering or personal vendettas – something much more important was at stake.

The diverse group, united by their common goal, set out on foot towards Gastovia Castle. As the sun beat down on their backs, Auorak estimated they had about half a day's journey ahead of them. The once distant howling of wolves now echoed through the trees, their haunting cries like an unwelcome symphony to the travelers' ears. The pack was serenading the arrival of the newborn prince, their wild voices carrying across the land.

The endless howls of the creatures outside echoed through the landscape, sending shivers down our spines. The sheer number of them made their hearts race with fear. Drak, his face grim and determined as he silently prayed for a miracle. Their fates lay in the hands of the gods now as the darkness closed in around us, suffocating any hope we had left.

The towering castle loomed in the distance, its grey stone walls reaching up to pierce the sky. Bathed in the deep red light of the rising Blood Moon, it seemed both majestic and foreboding.

As they made their final trek towards the castle gates, each member of the group couldn't help but wonder what awaited them within those ancient walls. Would it be a place of wonder and enchantment, welcomed by their dear friend, or a dark and treacherous place destined to be their tomb?

The air was thick with anticipation as they approached, their hearts pounding in time with their footsteps. The castle seemed to stare down at them, challenging them to enter its mysterious depths. The wind carried a faint whisper, almost like a warning, but they pressed on, for they had come too far to turn back now.

Gastovia Castle

As the group neared, the ancient drawbridge fell with a thunderous crash. A lone figure emerged from the shadows of the entrance, their silhouette illuminated by the eerie red glow of the moon. It was Val, his human form barely containing the powerful aura that radiated from him. His chest rose and fell with each deep breath, his muscles taut and ready for action.

The air around him crackled with energy, hinting at his true nature as a shapeshifter. But for now, he appeared fully human, a mere mortal in this world of magic and mystery.

The relief in Val's voice was palpable as he spoke to the group. His eyes gleamed with gratitude as he gestured towards the castle where Nephrym and their newborn child were resting, his body still recovering from the birth. "He has asked about you all multiple times," he added with a smile.

"I assure you, he will be fine." A sense of excitement filled her words as she continued, "I cannot wait for you to meet our son, Val'Nevrin." The name rolled off his tongue like a precious gem, and it was clear that this child already held a special place in his heart. "Come now, rest, and I will take you to Nephrym first thing in the morning."

Their footsteps echoed loudly as they crossed the threshold of the castle walls, unaware of the horrors that lurked within. The demons and the wolves were now truly one. The Blood Moon loomed ominously above them, a foreboding omen of the terror that awaited in the Land of Dodd. Little did they know, this was only the beginning.

To Be Continued

www.ingramcontent.com/pod-product-compliance
Lightning Source LLC
Chambersburg PA
CBHW031322170626
46807CB00002B/533